Negotiation
The Snows of Windroven

Two Stories of The Twelve Kingdoms and The Uncharted Realms

by Jeffe Kennedy

"Negotiation" first appeared in *Thunder on the Battlefield*, Volume II, ed. James R. Tuck. 2013. Seventh Star Press, pp. 5-43.
"The Snows of Windroven" first appeared in *Amid the Winter Snow: A Holiday Anthology*. 2017.

Thank you for reading!

<u>Credits</u>
Content Editor: Peter Senftleben (The Snows of Windroven)
Line and Copy Editor: Rebecca Cremonese (The Snows of Windroven); James R. Tuck (Negotiation)
Back Cover Copy: Erin Nelsen Parekh (The Snows of Windroven)
Cover Design: Ravven (www.ravven.com)

Table of Contents

NEGOTIATION

A Story of the Twelve Kingdoms

by Jeffe Kennedy

A wounded warrior trapped by the sorceress who knows him better than he does himself…

General Uorsin escapes the last devastating battle, only to find himself alone on a mountain, feverish and no closer to finding the paradise that drives him on. Salena, greatest shapeshifter and magic-worker of her people, springs the trap she's set to protect her land—and to prevent the ravager Uorsin from ever reaching it.

Together, they spend a night setting the terms that will determine not only the rest of their lives, but the fates of the peoples of the Twelve Kingdoms—and the thirteenth.

———————————

S ALENA DIDN'T NEED to smell the blood to know the warrior was wounded.

It showed in the sag of his body, the way he cradled his side, curling over it with that animal instinct to present the ridged spine to the cruel world, protecting the soft underbelly.

Nothing he did would protect him from her.

She hung back in the shadowy grove, letting the snowfall muffle her scent and the stark lines of the forest disguise her shape. After so much watching and waiting, the moment was finally upon her.

The man swayed in the saddle, barely conscious. His will, however, penetrated his fevered mind to keep him clinging to his horse while the stallion carried him to the one place Salena could never allow him to go.

None of this surprised her.

Very little did, really. Which could be both good and bad.

In this case, only one real question remained. Which would this be?

She'd seen this moment coming for most of her life. This pivot point for so many fates arrowing in from the beyond, like a meteor set in motion eons ago, just now hurtling into physical view. From her dome under the sea, her sacred seat of power, the images had played out for her, all the futures equally possible until the moment of decision, when the pattern of events became inevitable.

For years she'd examined the outcomes, unable to discern which of her actions would trigger each. Now the moment was upon her. The next choices would set the course for her beloved land of Annfwn, for the larger world and, not incidentally, her own fate.

Nothing would stop this meteor of destiny and the resulting destruction. All any of them could do was choose the point of impact. And by any of them, that meant Salena, because she was the only one who knew.

She'd made her first choice already, just by being here. The warrior must not be allowed to enter Annfwn.

The stallion nickered nervously, rolling an eye in her direction. Not seeing her yet, but catching her scent perhaps. Or just sensing the presence of death, the predator in the forest. She padded nearer, the horse dancing aside, into the deeper snow off the path.

The warrior grunted, pain jouncing him into greater awareness, his hand going even now to his sword hilt, as if he could swing it. He would be easy to kill. In her wolf form, she could overmatch the weakened man. His blood would run hot and sweet in her mouth and so many things would never happen. Especially for her. Her life would be reasonably good if he died now, alone in this forest he should never have entered. A short-term solution, oh so tempting in its simplicity. More, the outcome beckoned—Salena would live out her days in Annfwn, perhaps not happily, but not in misery.

It galled her to see past the short-term, to the chaos of civil war, the death, disease and starvation that would grow so large that the festering would eat into Annfwn itself. Not tomorrow. Not next year. Probably not even in her lifetime. Another woman would have pretended not to see it, would have turned her face away and enjoyed the now for what it was.

Salena herself would have done it, before her baby died. Before Tosin took the coward's way out and killed himself.

Grief taught you things.

Salena would never again ignore the portents, never again place blind faith in joy.

She slunk closer, letting the horse sense her now, the glimpse of a fang in the shadows, not too much. Just a hint of canine musk, of danger. Not this path. That way, towards the only choice she could make—saving the man who would be her slow destruction.

THE PAIN WORKED on him like a dull knife. He fancied he felt shards of broken ribs shredding his liver, gutting him while he lived. It wasn't real. He knew that much from years of cleaning fish and other beasts. Only the skin and muscles feel. Nothing ever flinches when you slice the internal organs. Only man, and only because he's cursed with imagination.

His mount stumbled through the deep snow, staggering precariously over buried limbs and Uorsin swore, blinking against the snowfall. The creature must scent a predator, to choose such a trail, moving in such a panic. He scanned the columns of trees, black against the greys of winter-shrouded slanted land, uncertain where he'd been carried in his delirium. Battle haze obscured the details—pretty Castle Columba in the distance with her deceptively low walls and scholarly occupants.

It should have been an easy victory, but the siege had taken too long. He'd underestimated, an error that gnawed at him, the pain nearly as great as the sword he'd taken to the side, coming up from under his fighting arm, piercing him before he saw the movement.

He gripped the reins, trying to steady the horse's headlong plunge through treacherous deadfall. There had been a path. They must return to it. Through force of will, he guided the horse back the way they'd come.

Where had he been going? Somewhere important. Important enough for him to make those cringing bastards at Columba patch him up with the simple bandage that clearly wasn't enough.

He hadn't counted on the fever taking him.

A soft growl echoed over the crack of the horse's hooves on deadfall, the hairs rising on the back of his neck. He flexed his sword arm, testing the strength he'd built since childhood, hauling fishing nets and climbing between boat and surf. Who knew being a fisherman's son trained you to be a warrior? That strength failed him now. He could not face down a wolf. And where there was one, there would certainly be a pack.

But they would not go downhill.

Turning his mount away from the sound and scent of wild beast, he leaned forward in the saddle, willing the horse's hooves to find purchase. It scrabbled willingly, grateful to move away from the danger.

Uorsin clenched his teeth against the chattering waves of fever. Perhaps he should have waited to heal, as Derodotur had urged him. They'd taken Castle Columba only to find themselves under siege in turn. One they'd hopefully withstand better than the foolish Mailloux family had, despite their unexpected luck.

And then—yes, that healer woman—she'd told him the story of paradise, just over the hill. *Annfwn.* A land where the sea lapped like warm honey on white sugar sand. More beautiful than Elcinea, better fortified than Avonligdh, richer than Duranor.

Full of magic.

Others would scoff, but Uorsin knew the fishermen's tales of the golden land over the sea that couldn't be sailed. A land of limitless abundance where the sun never set and the fruits hung heavy on the trees all year round.

Glorianna the Good knew they needed resources. Duranor's long gambit to solidify its hold on its neighbors stood on weakened legs. Winter had set in with an early vicious swipe that left Uorsin's armies isolated, cut off from supply chains. They could not win while splintered into miserable huddles of starving soldiers.

Annfwn.

This was the golden prize he sought. He felt it in his bones. Even as a young lad, the stories and songs swept him up, stirring a longing in him that he couldn't define, would never explain. He had to go there. Real or imagined.

And to think it lay just over this hill, an actual place over a simple mountain pass. He hadn't waited another moment. Annfwn—and all her lush glories—would belong to him.

THE WARRIOR PROVED stubborn, but this also was no surprise to Salena. If he didn't have that quality, that double-face of will and obstinacy, he wouldn't be such a threat.

She slipped through the trees, letting her scent fall through the moist air to the already skittish horse. The poor beast feared its rider more than her, however, and struggled on. Time to change things up.

Stilling, she gathered her magic, pulling it into her core and letting it flow out again into a new form. Her talons gripped the icy rock and she mantled her wings, testing them. She never changed into an imperfect form. Her father would never have allowed the slightest error. Perfection became a habit over time, even with no one watching.

She launched herself from the rock, a black slash of raptor plummeting from the cliff side overhead. With a bloodcurdling scream no normal bird could produce, she stooped low over horse and rider, taking feral pleasure in the man's startled cry, which became a cry of pain when the horse wheeled, taking him in a plunging ride back down the mountain.

Yes, Uorsin. Feel that? That's a taste of all the misery you will give me.

Wings working against the heavy damp, she spiraled up, circling to see horse and rider fighting each other. If she could have cackled to herself, she would have, for they headed exactly for the cave she had in mind.

All Uorsin needed was a bit more incentive.

She landed and stilled. For months she'd conserved her energy for this, pulling from Annfwn's rich supply of mother magic. Shapechanging away outside her homeland's borders took more effort, but not so much that she couldn't slide easily into a third form. These were all her favorites, but this one—the saber-toothed black cat—this was the best.

Prowling behind, letting out low coughs of warning, she drove the desperate pair into shallower snow.

See? This way is much easier.

The horse, finding firmer footing, pulled ahead and she let it take the lead, especially with them so firmly headed for the cave she'd prepared.

Now for one more transformation.

And the final trick.

THE CAVE SEEMED too good to be true. Which meant it was.

Uorsin eyed it with deep suspicion and even more profound exhaustion. The stallion shuddered under him, the animal succumbing to the chill that fingered into its sweating hide. If he didn't give the horse a rub down and a chance to rest, it would founder, leaving Uorsin to carry his treasure on foot.

Not an acceptable option.

Besides which, he needed to rest and eat. Perhaps wait out this blizzard and give his wounds a chance to heal. Steeling himself, he nearly crawled off the horse, managing not to collapse in the snow by clinging to the saddle in a most undignified way.

The horse danced sideways under his leaning weight, turning to eye the forest. Something out there, stalking them both. He shook off the vague fear that the cave might be a trap. At least it would be defensible. If he died here, the songsters would say that the General of Duranor's forces disappeared into the Wild Lands following a crushing defeat.

There could be worse tales. Nobody sang about a crippled ex-warrior of a vanquished land.

Now—if he survived the night and made his way to Arnfwn—there would be a grand story. And his destiny, he felt it in his bones.

The shadows of the cave wrapped around them as he led the

steed inside, only somewhat less dark than the failing light outside. Some helpful someone had stacked kindling and larger pieces of wood. A clean firepit showed signs of previous use, but nothing so obviously convenient as a fire-striker.

He unsaddled the horse and unloaded the necessary camping supplies, making quick work of getting the fire going—and, not incidentally, illuminate the cave and discourage any nasty denizens.

With his horse rubbed down and contently dozing, Uorsin settled himself by the fire to gnaw on his usual field rations and kept an eye on the mouth of the cave, his sword and dagger beside him. The ache from his reopened wound served to keep him awake and alert.

With the anticipation of a man addicted to battle, he awaited whoever had set him up.

SHE MISSED THE cat's body immediately. Truly, any of her animal forms would be preferable, like wearing a weapon instead of relying upon the simple dagger at her hip. If all went as she'd planned so meticulously, she wouldn't need to physically defend herself. After all, he was only a man. And a mossback at that. If necessary, she could shapeshift in an instant to defend herself. But that would defeat her purpose.

Her goals required the oldest tricks. Not attack, but seduction.

So she took some care with her appearance—something she hadn't done since Tosin died, she realized with a dull pang of moldy grief—using the supplies she'd stowed away. All men were the same in the end. A revealing dress, a bit of makeup and long, loose hair.

Maybe her first offer would suffice.

She paused at the mouth of the cave, letting him study her. She'd thought he might be sleeping, exhausted from his wounds and the adrenaline-spiked chase through the woods. But he sat upright, fist wrapped around the hilt of a sword she knew he could barely lift. Interesting that he still chose his dominant arm. The left hand draped casually next to a hunting knife. A decoy, then.

His fair hair glinted in the firelight, chin stubbled. He hadn't traveled that long, so clearly it was more that he didn't care for appearances. If she made him High King, he'd had have to change that.

She'd considered her first words to him. Playing coy was never much of a possibility—fun as it might have been to toy with him. From what she'd seen, his savvy as a strategist would cut through any dissembling on her part. Already, she sensed the cogs and wheels of his thoughts assembling the pieces, determining who she must be.

Stepping into the cave far enough so the fire would show her features, Salena slipped back her hood and let her lips curve into a smile to stir even the most cynical groin.

"Greetings General Uorsin. I am Salena of the Tala. I'm here to give you your greatest desire."

THE WITCH HAD balls, he'd give her that. Or perhaps that was the wrong word. She smiled with all the smoky sweetness of a woman offering a night of pleasure, but under it ran the glint of steel.

Uorsin loved a challenge.

"Sit then, Salena of the Tala. Share my fire—which I have no doubt you arranged—and tell me how you plan to deliver Annfwn into my hands."

She lowered her chin. "Annfwn is a myth."

"You offered my heart's desire and that is Annfwn. I don't care if others think it's a myth. I know what my gut tells me." He hadn't gotten where he was by letting others tell him how the world worked.

"It hardly seems rational to set your sights on something so…ephemeral."

"And yet, here I sit, trapped in cave during a blizzard by animals that seemed to intelligently hunt me down. Does that fit your definition of rational?"

She tilted her head, the way a cat might to judge distance, and he found himself bracing for attack, the sound of that predatory jaguar's cough echoing in his mind. Her shining dark hair shone with red and her skin looked pale as the snow she'd stepped out of.

"Annfwn is a dream. I'm here to offer you reality."

"Who are the Tala? I've never heard of these people you supposedly claim."

She lifted one shoulder, the movement raising her full breasts under the cloak, drawing his eye like a starving dog's to the haunch of beef just outside its kennel. Lust had lowered many a man. He would do well to keep that in mind.

"Does it truly matter which people I claim? I don't think so, General Uorsin."

"If you mean to make me uneasy by making it clear you know who I am, you have failed. The people of the Twelve Kingdoms have all heard of me by now."

"But the Tala are not of the Twelve Kingdoms," she said.

"Neither is Annfwn."

"How can it be when it doesn't exist?"

He found his lips twitching in an unexpected desire to grin at her. "Exactly."

She might be dangerous as all hell, and probably a witch or something worse—whatever that might be—but a fair opponent presented certain delights beyond the pleasures of the flesh or the battle. Uorsin gestured to the opposite side of the fire.

"Sit, Witchwoman, and make your offer. I am intrigued what you think might tempt my heart away from the fabled paradise of Annfwn."

IT MADE NO sense for her, however grudgingly, to like him. Of course, he wasn't as bad now as he would become. Something of the gentle seas of Elcinea clung to him still at this point in his young life, the simplicity of the working man. He hadn't yet drunk enough of the power that would ultimately corrupt him.

She sat, tucking the cloak demurely around her knees, pulling out the long fall of her hair and draping it over her shoulder, so he might better eye the gleaming sweep of it. He had his eye on her, oh yes, flicking down to catch what curves he could see.

"You are a beautiful woman." He threw it out as a statement, nearly a challenge. As if acknowledging an opponent with a strong sword arm.

"I know."

"Most ladies would play coy, demur, pretend to be embarrassed."

Ah, and here he truly thought to flatter her. "I am no lady—

make no mistake there."

He grunted and stirred the fire, making the flames jump. "I shall not fall into the trap of asking what you really are."

"You don't talk like a sailor."

"Another gambit to hint how much more you know about me. What is it you're really trying to tell me, Salena of the nonexistent Tala?"

"That I do know more than you do. Because of that I can help you, Uorsin, late of Elcinea, failed leader of Duranor's now decimated forces."

The blood leapt under the thin skin of his broad cheekbones, that anger flaring like the flames between them. Over and over, she'd seen in her visions how the rage drove him—out of his poor fishing village, into greater and more important roles in the war, a strategist and blood fury warrior. It would also drive him—and all the Thirteen Kingdoms, counting Annfwn—into shattered fragments of what could have been. The double-edged blade that could unite or destroy.

And both at once.

"What?" She needled him with her mocking tone. "Did I speak an untruth—or can you not bear to face what is real?"

"I know the truth!" His hand flexed on the hilt of the sword by his side, a grimace of pain glancing over his face. Pain from the wound or of the defeated general—which was worse? "Believe me, Witch, you cannot know what it's like to watch your troops die because of your failure. To see your own dreams and the dreams of millions crumble to dust along with it. Foolish is the warrior who cannot recognize when he is vanquished."

"Then you have surrendered?" She knew he hadn't, but she wanted to plant that word in his mind.

"No." He said it softly, releasing his grip on the hilt to stroke it with near affection, then flicked his eyes up to her. "That's why I want Annfwn."

"You will never have it."

"WHO ARE YOU to say so?"

"I've already told you."

Which told him nothing, as she knew perfectly well. She looked beyond beautiful in the firelight. Uncannily so. She was probably the most gorgeous woman he'd ever seen for himself, like an image from one of Glorianna's chapels. No, not Glorianna, with her sunshine and pink roses. This woman would be in one of Moranu's night temples, moonlight and shrouded in shadow, her flame-black hair blending with the night and those storm grey eyes full of knowingness, like the goddess herself.

Something about her too, made the small hairs on his arms stand on end, as if a lightning bolt poised to strike nearby. His own unease irritated him. He'd left those superstitions behind with the nets and the fish and the ceaseless, meaningless toil.

He wanted her, though, on a visceral level, with a deep craving that alarmed him more than any other part of this. Lust meant nothing. More—it could be a trap. Like all of this.

"You've told me nothing of any significance, except that you intend to keep me from Annfwn."

"That is the salient point."

"To your mind," he said.

"My mind is the one that matters."

"And why is that, Witch?"

"Why do you call me 'witch'?"

He leaned back on his good elbow, drawing the sword with

him and stretching his legs out. Full night had fallen outside, but a flurry of snowflakes blowing a good arm's length into the cave showed that the blizzard raged on. "Because," he watched her face, "you make my skin crawl."

That serene expression didn't flicker, but her full lips tensed, ever so slightly. A hit.

"And what do you imagine I can do?" She dropped her tone. Bed-voiced, trying to seduce him. He cut short those images she so deliberately stirred in his mind.

"Other than command beasts of the forest to drive a man's steed into a frenzy so that he's trapped in a cave while you work your wiles?" He laughed. "Isn't that enough?"

The satisfied glimmer in her eyes did not escape his notice. She could do much more than that. He leaned forward on his elbow, ignoring the twinge in his side. "Or is there more—perhaps you muddle my mind, making me want you."

She didn't smile, like a court woman would. Instead she returned his scrutiny with grave intensity. "And do you want me, Uorsin?"

"A man would have to be half dead not to."

"Ah, but aren't you half dead? Even now your wound festers, poisoning your blood." Her nostrils flared, like an animal's scenting prey. The unconscious reflex sent atavistic shivers down his spine. "Maybe I should let you climb the mountain. You might well die on the way, having never reached Annfwn."

"Which doesn't exist," he reminded her.

"It is a myth," she replied.

"I am not half dead."

"No." She did smile then, a cruel and taunting twist to that full mouth. "Which means I cannot let you climb this mountain."

"Are you offering me yourself instead?"

Her smile widened, showing a glimpse of teeth brushing her bottom lip. "Would that suffice?"

"Do you compare your worth to paradise?"

"Let's see, shall we?" She rose to her feet, a boneless unspooling, and unfastened her cloak, letting it drop like shed skin around her.

Her naked body glowed as if lit from within, breasts full and waist narrow. She was no unspoiled maid, but full woman. Feral. Sexual. His cock hardened, draining the blood from his head. Fool.

"What do you think?" Her mouth lifted on one side, well aware of her effect on him.

"I am no idiot youth to be overcome by the sight of a woman's nakedness. I am a man and a warrior." It was true. He despised those men who claimed to be swept away by desire for a woman's sweet limbs, who used that as an excuse not to control themselves in the most basic way. "I can want without acting."

She raised one eyebrow and shook her hair back, bending to don the cloak again and sitting as before. "I do admire your will, Uorsin. It's quite your most redeeming quality, in truth."

IT HAD BEEN worth a try.

And good for her, to practice being vulnerable to him. No man had seen her naked since Tosin and it was time to lay that in the grave along with him. He'd taken the coward's way out, too weak to face the pain of living. She would not fold like he had. Her duty—her sacred obligation—required her to soldier on.

Her lonely army of one.

"So what else do you offer me?" Stretched out as he was, Uorsin was not unappealing, with his long legs and broad shoulders. She could stomach bedding him, despite his brutal streak. Long enough for her purposes, anyway. "I assume the use of your body remains on the table."

Cad. His satisfied smirk confirmed it. It seemed to be wound into the male psyche—use her sexuality as a lever, try to make her feel like nothing more than a tool. She laughed and shook her hair back. "You wish, General. Let's make something clear right now. No matter what other terms we settle upon, I will never be something you use. Not tonight. Not tomorrow. Not until the day I pass from this body forever."

"You speak of years." He frowned, discomfort deeper than his wound.

"Yes." She held his gaze. This would be a deciding moment. "Yes—what we are deciding tonight is your future and mine. Our shared destiny, if you will. Our mated fates, if you won't."

"What's the difference?"

If he only knew. What a blessing it would be, not to know. Seeing future suffering meant you felt the pain in your bones, the anticipation as grinding as grief over the past.

"My own vision of the world. For me, destiny is good fortune. Fate is doom."

"I don't believe in either."

"You don't have to."

"Yet you're asking me to make decisions now—not just choices, but lasting vows—based on some vague predictions of the future.”

“Not vague!” She snapped the words out, her own temper rising. Galling that this mossback could not come close to understanding the searing reality of the visions she'd seen. That future devastation was as tangible to her as the sword lying by his side and he dismissed her warnings. The anger might be his fatal flaw, but this—this total disregard that other people possessed understanding he did not—this made him capable of so much destruction. Forever a careless boy in his mind, he would never gain the true maturity needed for the position he'd rise to.

He could only be moderated, for a time.

“You want proof, ignorant mossback? When you were nine, you killed your sister's cat, just to see what would happen.”

Shock—and a slice of horror—crawled over his face. “That's a lie! No one could know that.”

She allowed herself to smile at his inadvertent confession. “No—because you threw the cat's body into the sea, didn't you? When the tide was going out, so there'd be no danger of it washing up again.”

He'd levered himself into a sitting position while she spoke, eyes flicking to the mouth of the cave, as if he might escape.

“You *are* a witch.”

“No, but close enough. I saw you do that, just as I've seen the other heinous things you've done and the worse things you will do, if I don't stop you.”

“Stop me? With what—these stories. Dread tales of the future?” He sneered, taking refuge in scorn. “What—will you fuck me to death?”

"No," she leaned forward, letting the cloak slide open enough for one bare leg to slide through, "the fucking will be to keep you content and give us heirs. I have other ways of making sure you don't cross any sacred lines ever again."

"Killing a cat is hardly sacred."

"That you think so is what makes you a brute."

"I've done far worse." He flung that at her, as if to shock her.

She tilted her head and tapped her temple, reminding him. "I know."

His mind churned, a bubbling pit of dark anger, shame and secrets like rotting meat falling from the bone. At last, she'd made her point.

FEAR CHOKED IN his throat. And he was not a man to feel fear. He'd seen it in others, but always as a sign of weakness. Fear came from lack of confidence. Somehow this witch, this snake of a woman had crawled beneath his guard and undermined him. She had to die. Not just for that, but because she knew too much.

A slim thing, leanly muscled—she couldn't be that strong or trained in battle. Even in his weakened state, he could take her.

With a roar meant to startle thought from her prescient brain, he leapt across the fire, strong-heeled boots crushing the embers, bringing his broad-bladed hunting knife up in an uppercut that would drive through her fragile ribcage and into her black witch's heart.

Those storm-grey eyes flashed diamond bright, not in shock or terror, but in . . . triumph?

The thought barely registered before he was on her, the blade slicing through the air where she'd been.

He rolled, his wound splitting open.

No, that was the slice of claws.

The liquid snarl of the jaguar pierced his skull even as the jaws fastened on his throat, razor claws dug deep into his shoulders and back haunches poised to eviscerate his vulnerable belly.

It was *her*.

His thoughts jangled around the idea. She became the cat. She didn't control the forest animals, she was them.

And he was dead.

Only he wasn't. The moment stretched out with timeless intensity. The hot breath on his throat, the nauseating feel of those claws deep in muscle that should never feel such a thing. She could have disemboweled him with one careless kick of her hind leg, but she had not. She was waiting.

"I surrender." He barely gasped out the words, the shame of his easy defeat paling against the desire to live through this night.

She released him, moving her crushing weight with a single graceful leap. The jaguar sat, gazing at him with unnatural bright-blue eyes, like jewels. She licked her chops, clearing away the blood. His blood.

He tried to sit, but failed, the blood seeping from his shoulders and opened wound, draining his head, leaving only blackness behind.

THAT HAD GONE very well.

Salena busied herself while Uorsin was unconscious, unpacking the supplies she'd hidden in the back of the cave. Such was the value of foresight. The upside of dealing with such a predictable man was that every possible scenario had shown him trying to kill her. She shook her head to herself. He'd thought so little of her that she'd seen it coming for long moments before he moved. Unlikely she'd have that advantage ever again.

She donned her working clothes, ones she didn't mind getting some blood on, and set out her tools and potions. Then she sat beside him and waited for him to wake up. Healing him could happen without his being conscious, but she wanted him to ask for it.

Beg a little.

Something for her to remember when things got bad.

Unlike other men, he didn't look younger or sweeter asleep. Even unconscious, he reminded her of the bear he was named for. Hibernating, perhaps, and all the deadlier should you awaken him.

He groaned before opening his eyes, pressing a hand to his side. His gaze fastened on her—fear and disgust quickly buried by that anger. It galvanized him, a meaty hand reaching for her throat before he remembered how things stood.

She raised an eyebrow at him, deliberately cool.

"What are you?" He ground it out, a demand for information.

"I told you. I am Tala."

"You're a demon."

"You believe in demons?"

"No, but I don't believe in shapeshifters either." He stared at the ceiling. "It was you in the forest."

"Yes."

"The eagle."

"More of a large hawk, but yes."

"Can you be any animal?"

"I'm more practiced at some than others, but theoretically, yes."

He rolled his head and eyed her. "That cat was bigger than you are."

"Yes. Size is irrelevant."

"How can that be?"

This still gave her pleasure, a small measure of joy. She allowed herself to grin at him. "Magic."

"And you magicked those clothes, too?"

"I can take clothes with me when I shift, but no—I had these already stowed in the cave."

"You saw all of this, beforehand."

"Yes."

HE'D BEEN CLEANLY outmaneuvered. It didn't take much of a strategist to recognize that.

A sick despair preyed through his soul that he might die here. All his bold dreams of glory, of a better life, crumpled into nothingness. Worse—it would look like he'd slunk off the battlefield and ended his own life rather than face his superiors or a world where he shared Duranor's final defeat. It rankled that he'd be thought a coward.

But, between the wounds, the blood loss and his deadly captor—for surely there was no better word for her—he could not survive this. Why did she delay the inevitable?

"Why didn't you just kill me in the forest?" He spoke wearily to the shadowed ceiling, unable to bear looking at her again.

"Why the elaborate charade?"

Her hesitation was palpable. Already he began to know her, those pauses when she chose which words to prick him with.

"I wanted to. I still want to."

"Comforting."

"Coming from the man who just tried to kill me."

"True." He breathed out the pain. "But?"

She moved, a bare rustle of fabric, and came to lean over him, her dark red hair falling down to shadow her face. "Listen to me very closely. This is important. If you live, I can make you not only a victor of Duranor's ill-advised conquest, but High King of the Twelve Kingdoms. You can end this endless conflict and bring the next best thing to peace to the realm. For that reason, and for that reason only, I have not killed you as I so long to do." She stroked his cheek in a strange parody of affection, her hand cool on his fevered skin, her grey eyes intent. No sweetness in her. Had there ever been? It seemed impossible that she had ever been a young girl.

"What do you care? The Tala—if they exist—are not among the Twelve Kingdoms."

She smiled, as if tucking a secret behind her lips. "My reasons are my own."

"I will be king of nothing if I die in this cave."

"Ah yes." She slid her hand down to the claw marks carved into his shoulder, watching his face to see him flinch. "Would you like me to heal you?"

"Can you?"

"Yes." She prodded the wound and he clenched his teeth to keep from showing her how much it hurt. "If you agree to my terms."

"You are a cruel woman."

"Yes. A fit queen for a brute like you."

It took him by surprise, choking his breath in his throat, making him cough. Which sent agonies through his belly. This was torture, he realized. Subtly arranged, but torture nonetheless.

"That's what this is about?" he asked, when he regain himself. "Power? You'll make me High King just so you can be queen?"

"I thought it might be a motivation you'd understand." She tucked her hair behind her ears and sat back on her heels. "These are my terms: I will heal you now. I will offer the services of the Tala to win your war. I will become your queen and give you three heirs."

She tapped him on the nose and he felt like biting off her finger.

"All you have to do is beg me for it."

HE HATED HER in that moment. It shone clearly on his face and the satisfaction rippled through her.

That's right, my brutal husband, hate me now so I will always know where I stand with you.

"I will never beg." He wouldn't look at her, clinging to his pride, even as he lay at her mercy. She'd known when she made her plan that he would never forget that she'd brought him to this, that she always could. It would be vital for their marriage, that he would always know, despite the vast power he would attain and wield like the sword forgotten on the other side of the fire, that *she* could bring him to this.

She would comfort herself with that in the long days ahead.

"Beg me," she commanded him. "Or I won't."

His fever-bright eyes caught hers and he grinned, a baring of his teeth. "Oh, yes you will. Because you don't want me to die. Whatever your mysterious reasons—and I don't for one bleeding moment believe you want peace for a realm that isn't yours—it's enough to bring you here, to make this bargain. I don't want a queen, or a wife, for that matter."

"But you do want to live, don't you, Uorsin?" She coaxed him with her voice, a minor power of persuasion, but a handy one. "Think of all that awaits you. You could be High King. Not bad for a simple fisherman from sleepy Elcinea. Nothing would be beyond your reach."

"One thing." He fixed her with that obstinate stare. "Annfwn."

Yes. That was the reason for all of it. She would give anything to protect her sacred home. Would give everything. And the healthy babes he'd give her would return to Annfwn someday and keep it safe and whole forever.

Uorsin didn't need to know that they would be all girls.

A nice little surprise for the future.

"What do you care for a mythical paradise when you can have all the world?"

His face changed and suddenly he looked like the youth, the innocent that even unconsciousness hadn't brought to him. A yearning showed through him, released perhaps by the fever. His eyes brightened with unshed tears.

"I don't know," he whispered it, almost to himself. "I just wanted to see it—at least once."

"It's not for you." She layered all her powers of suggestion into her words. "But you can have everything else."

"Have you seen it?" He asked her with near childish urgency. She would have to heal him soon, regardless, before the fever took him down much more. "I just wanted to see it!"

Moved by a surprising stab of sympathy, she laid a hand over his. "No," she lied. "Annfwn is a myth."

He sighed, disappointment creasing his face, eyes closing on his resignation. Then he opened them again, scrutinizing her with his familiar canniness. "High King, you say?"

"Yes. High King of the Twelve Kingdoms."

"Plus three heirs and the most beautiful woman I've ever seen as my queen? Along with my life?"

"Yes."

"You've seen all this, in your crystal ball or your tea leaves?"

"So to speak. For the third time—yes."

"I won't be a kind husband. Don't delude yourself of that. You don't deserve that from me."

"I know." Better than he did.

"And there will always be other women. You won't be enough for me. You, however, must be faithful, so I'll be certain the babes are mine."

"I know that, too."

"You are a fool to agree to these terms."

Perhaps that was so. She'd always thought martyrs were fools. Now she understood—martyring yourself was what you did when you had nothing left. When you gambled the pitiful lot you had left hoping that your nothing life would at least mean something in the end.

See, Tosin? I'm committing suicide too. At least mine will serve the Tala and Annfwn.

"I AM A fool," she agreed easily. Too easily. Every bone in his body told him that she had other motives. That she was using him. She didn't care about being queen. Power recognizes power. He knew it in a man, selecting the ones to lead. And he knew it in women, watching for the ones who sought to use him. There's a certain hunger that shows in the eyes. She didn't have it.

She hungered for something else.

"What else?"

She raised an eyebrow at him, pretending not to know what he meant. But, oh no, he wasn't so far gone that he didn't know there was something more.

"There's something you want from all this, Salena, and I don't kid myself that you crave my cock and the throne beside me. It's the babes, isn't it?"

Aha! He'd surprised her there. The flicker in those inscrutable grey eyes. She sighed a little.

"One of the babes, yes, whichever bears my stamp. That child will return to the Tala."

"One of three, eh?" He mulled it over. "The witch child."

She nodded, prickled and he enjoyed that he'd gotten this upper hand. Then an unsettling thought occurred to him. "Will they be shapeshifters—like you? My children will be monsters?"

Now she glared in truth, but didn't rise to his bait. "One of them will carry my stamp and will have the gift of shifting. One will be your heir, nearly your mirror. And the third…"

He waited, caught up despite himself. When she got that faraway look, seeing something beyond the walls of the cave, she looked like the goddess he'd first thought her to be. As if lit from within by some pure flame.

Like he'd imagined Annfwn to be.

"Yes?" He prompted her. "The third?"

She started a little, gaze focusing back on this world. She lifted one shoulder in a shrug and smiled at him, the echo of affection for someone else still on her lips. "Something in between."

"You will not teach them your witchy ways."

She sobered. "You cannot command that."

"I can." She'd tipped her hand all right. Her power might be great, but she'd never stood down a charge in battle. She knew nothing of negotiation, in the final analysis. It had been her fundamental mistake, to put him in this position, where he had nothing to lose and everything to gain. In the end, she wanted this more than he did.

Because he had to give up the one thing, the only thing he'd ever really wanted.

She dipped her chin, a bare nod of agreement.

"Heal me then. Make me strong, Witch, and then you and I shall set our terms."

Though he commanded instead of begged, she set to work. He savored her submission to his will. Even this most powerful witch needed him and would do what he told her.

He took that childish longing to see paradise and cut it from his heart.

SHE WOULDN'T CRY.

All her tears had been shed already, for the babe she'd lost, for Tosin's pointless death—and for her future.

She'd gotten exactly what she'd wanted and that would have to be enough. One couldn't have it all—not even Uorsin. Working over his broad torso, she repaired the body of the man who would be her last. That flesh, the toughened skin over warrior's muscle and sturdy bones—it would give her strong daughters. The daughters the Tala deserved and could not breed on their own.

Ironic that fate dictated it should be him. That the Tala blood running in his veins would be enough to give him the longing for—and the entry to—Annfwn. But that it fell short of giving him the nature to protect it. Not all with the ability to enter Annfwn were worthy of it. The magic couldn't understand that.

But she could.

She regretted, on one level, denying him a chance to see it. Blood called to blood and she understood how powerfully he longed for the homeland he'd never known. Perhaps if he'd made it to Annfwn sooner, it might have mellowed him, bled that anger and cruelty away. But it was far too late now.

He called her a monster, but the rapine was all in him. His nature was to devour. That could not be changed, only redirected.

The loss of Annfwn would harden his heart more and she accepted the burden of that guilt. The lesser of many potential evils.

Now, though—now the fragments reassembled into a new mosaic. The world she'd hoped for. Not perfect. The "peace" Uorsin would bring to the Twelve Kingdoms would be oppressive, but better than slaughter and chaos. Her own life would last not even twenty more years and would be a trial to her.

Her daughters, though, they would be her joy. They would return to safe and sacred Annfwn for her and give the Tala what she could not.

A future.

One of infinite possibilities.

The Snows of Windroven

A Twelve Kingdoms/Uncharted Realms Novella

by Jeffe Kennedy

A new power is at work in the Twelve Kingdoms, unbalancing the fragile peace. For the High Queen and her sisters, it might mean a new alliance—or the end of the love of a lifetime…

As a howling blizzard batters the mountain keep of Windroven, Ami, Queen of Avonlidgh, and her unofficial consort Ash face their own storm. Their passion saved them from despair, but Ash knows a scarred, jumpy ex-convict isn't the companion his queen needs. He's been bracing himself for the end since their liaison began. When it finally comes, the shattering of his heart is almost a relief.

With a man haunted by nightmares and silent as stone, Ami knows only that Ash's wounds are his own to hide or reveal. She can't command trust. But just as they are moving apart, a vicious attack confines them together, snowbound and isolated with an ancient force awakening within Windroven itself. If they truly mean to break their bond, Ami and Ash must first burn through a midwinter that will test every instinct—and bring temptation all too near…

Acknowledgements

Thanks to my Santa Fe critique group for terrific and extensive feedback on this story: Ed Khmara, Matt Reitan, Jim Sorenson, Sage Walker, and Eric Wolf.

Much gratitude to Thea Harrison for inviting me to be a part of this anthology, and to Grace Draven and Elizabeth Hunter, for joining in and making this project so much fun to do. You gals are awesome!

And many thanks, always, to Carien and David, for weekly calls and all the work you do.

~ 1 ~

"IF THERE IS some fire-breathing dragon beneath Windroven, maybe we won't need much wood for the fireplaces—natural heat!" Ami cast me a brilliant smile from the back of her horse. Probably hoping I'd be so dazzled by her playfulness, the mischief of her joke, that I wouldn't notice she was bent on cozening me into being happy about going to Windroven. I'd agreed—I had no choice, as there would be no winning this argument with her—but I wouldn't give in and let her charm me. This was a bad idea, and we all knew it.

I glanced back at the men-at-arms following in our compact procession, though Lieutenant Graves could no more change Ami's mind than I could. Even the twins, with terrible timing, were docile for once, providing no distraction from Ami's determined flirtation. I'd argued for a carriage for Ami and the toddlers to ride in for the journey from Castle Avonlidgh to Windroven, but Ami had dug in her heels. On that and everything else.

She might be my lover, but as the newly crowned Queen of Avonlidgh, she outranked me.

Stella rode in front of her mother in the saddle, the two of them wrapped in matching furred cloaks against the winter's chill—though the little girl kept pushing the hood back impatiently—and Astar rode in front of me, doing his best to drive my horse crazy by pulling at his mane by the fistful. During my time in Annfwn, the magic-filled homeland of my late father, who'd been full Tala, I'd learned a little mind-magic. As a part-blood I wasn't capable of much, but I had enough ability—I was strongest with animals—to keep a thread of soothing control on the horse's mind, despite Astar's worst efforts.

If only my internal beast could be so easily calmed. And if only I were better at steeling myself against Ami's gift for persuasion. In truth, she did dazzle me—simply by existing—much as I worked to toughen my hide against her charms. When she put real effort into it, I was a lost man. Redundant, as I was a lost man regardless.

Lost and broken beyond repair, even before Ami danced her way from my fantasies into passionate reality.

The old tales warn of the dangers of a man obtaining his heart's desire, how his fantasy should never come true lest he find his tragic fate in it. I'd thought I'd been careful, that I'd reminded myself enough times that Ami could never truly be mine, not for more than a brief while. But clearly my heart hadn't absorbed the lesson of those cautionary tales.

The story of my fucked-up life—I seemed to be determined to take the hardest road despite all warnings and good sense, every time.

"Glorianna willing," Ami continued doggedly, now pursing her rose-petal lips with sensuous intent, and sidling her steed closer to mine, "a dragon resident could melt all the snows and we'd have no winter at all! Wouldn't that be lovely?"

I resolutely looked away from her and her fierce beauty. Ami possesses Tala blood, too, though the royal kind, and though she can't shapeshift or perform sorcery, her magic manifests in her inhuman loveliness. She burns brighter than the sun, and if I allowed myself to fall into admiring her, my hapless brain tended to be seared of all rational thought.

"Good!" Ami chirped, an edge beneath the music. "I take it from your non-response that you're in total agreement with my plan. I'm so glad to hear it."

The Three curse it, now she'd cornered me. I couldn't leave it there.

"Going to Windroven is a terrible idea and you know it," I replied, studying the road ahead. We'd had fair travel thus far, but with all the strange monsters appearing around the Thirteen Kingdoms, it paid to keep alert. "Adequate firewood and snowfall will be the least of our worries."

She waved that off with a flick of her gloved fingers. "You only say that because you've never witnessed a Mornai storm at Windroven. They're spectacular. They blow in off the ocean, full of sea moisture. When the cold winds of the Northern Wastes hit them, the clouds turn heavy-bellied as a nine-months-pregnant woman—and just like that poor woman, they dump out snow in a torrent of afterbirth, deeper than a man can stand."

I swallowed the laugh that wanted to rise and gave her a stern look. She wasn't going to draw me out that way. "That's disgusting—and crude."

She blinked at me in contrived innocence, that practiced flutter of rose-gold lashes over the deep twilight blue of eyes the poets never seemed to tire of describing. "This from the man who taught me every crude word I know."

I sighed for the truth of that. "I'm well aware that I created a monster. But you're not distracting me. There's no reason we couldn't have stayed at Castle Avonlidgh, spent the Feast of

Moranu there. The whole winter, even."

"Ugh. I hate that place. I'm glad to be free of its gloomy walls. I handled the governmental minutiae and now court is on hiatus. Everyone is going home to spend the Feast of Moranu with their families and that's what I want, too. Andi is in Annfwn and Ursula is still off in the Nahanaun Islands, helping Dafne free her own dragon and whatever else all those letters are so carefully not saying. I might as well be in my own home."

"Castle Avonlidgh is as much your home now as Windroven."

"That's just not true." Ami's voice had gone serious, steel in it that so belied her frivolous exterior. "I don't expect you to understand, but from the first time Hugh brought me to Windroven, I felt at home there. He would have wanted the twins to winter at Windroven. It's their family's ancestral home and if all had been as it should, they would have spent their infancy there, taken their first steps on her stones, as all Avonlidgh's heirs have." Ami turned her smile on Stella, stroking the toddler's wild, dark curls. "Hugh might be gone, but I owe it to his memory to raise his children as he would have, had he lived."

Astar howled like a little wolf, then grinned, showing his few, decidedly unthreatening baby teeth. Ami smiled back at him, soft with maternal affection. It didn't help that I felt irrational jealousy for the golden prince who'd been so much more the right man for Ami, along with guilt that I not only bedded his wife, but helped raise his children. The noble Prince Hugh would likely be appalled that a part-blood Tala ex-convict had taken his place, even temporarily.

"I understand that." I did. I couldn't imagine the onus Ami must feel to honor the man she'd loved. "But you had a ball last night at Castle Avonlidgh. You could do the same all season—stay up all night drinking wine and dancing. You enjoy that well enough."

Ami shot me a dark look. "You're just jealous of all those men I danced with, which you shouldn't be."

A deadly hit there, as I was. Black jealousy that corroded my thoughts and best intentions. Where Ami was concerned, I lacked all reason and emotional control. I became the half-savage beast I'd been when I first heard a minstrel sing about the youngest and most beautiful daughter of the High King. I reverted to that feral creature who longed to disembowel every man who laid hands on her satin skin and devoured her with their eyes as if they owned her.

"You could have danced with me," Ami said, needling me, knowing exactly how to do it. "Then I wouldn't have *had* to dance with anyone else."

I didn't bother pointing out that a man at arms didn't dance with the Queen of Avonlidgh. Or that I couldn't stay alert and protect her if we danced. Or that I'd never learned how. In Ami's world, everyone learned to dance like they learned to walk. She forever forgot that we came from different worlds, whereas my burning shame forever reminded me of that unassailable fact.

I wouldn't let her see that embarrassment, however. Better for her to think me uninterested in dancing than for her to glimpse the rough and desperate boy inside.

"Talk to me, Ash," Ami commanded, all hint of flirtation vanished. "You know I hate it when you go all stoic White Monk on me."

I swallowed a terse retort to that, searching for a diplomatic reply. "Wintering at Windroven is a romantic idea, but romance won't last long if the volcano blows." I cleared my throat of the choking fear of losing her in such a way. I lived with that fear daily, knowing full well I had no business thinking of her as mine in the first place. I'd lose her eventually—today, next month, or next year—but sooner rather than later. Making myself confront the eventuality of our parting had become a kind of daily, disciplined exercise for me. Like sword practice. I forced myself to exercise the muscles of loss, to contemplate that pain. I could survive it, I thought, as long as she was alive and happy.

That's what I told myself. A constant mantra that did nothing to bring me peace.

As Queen of Avonlidgh, she'd have to marry for the good of the kingdom, and her future husband would hardly tolerate it if his beautiful new wife had a lover skulking in the shadows. Even if she didn't marry any time soon, the quiet gossip regarding my unsavory background would eventually grow loud enough to make her advisers insist on action. Most likely of all, Ami would simply wise up and realize her fling with a coarse, scarred, and broken man had been a fun excursion—a bit of dabbling in the crude underbelly of sex might be freeing for a time—but she would go back to her own kind. Back to a noble prince like Hugh had been. The sort of man who truly deserved her.

I was prepared for any of those scenarios. I'd rehearsed them in my mind so often that I knew all my lines by heart, just waiting for her to give me the correct cue.

What I couldn't bear was for her to be killed. Besides Annfwn, I'd found nothing and no one else that redeemed the cruelty and ugliness of the world. As long as Ami lived, so did my hope, fragile thing though it might be.

Ami was studying me now, her lovely blue eyes discerning too much. Since she'd given birth to the twins, she'd lost her ability to detect emotions—that gift belonged entirely to Stella, and the girl took it with her when she was born—but Ami retained some of that sensitivity by proximity. She also knew how to read and play me with Glorianna's own ruthless mastery of women over men.

"Ash." She spoke my name as she did during sex, and with that single scrape over my senses had my thoughts scattering on the cold winter winds.

"You *like* Windroven," she purred, effortlessly bringing to mind the few short days we'd spent there. She'd been still recovering from childbirth, but had been determined to use the time to practice her oral skills. For all that she looked the image of Glorianna as maiden, she'd embraced the earthiest of the goddess's personalities, exulting in the filthiest of sexual language, goading me into giving her more "cock-sucking lessons," knowing in her vixen's heart the hold she had on me.

I dispelled the images she evoked with a sharp shake of my head, resolutely staring at the road ahead. That's where my focus needed to be. Protecting my charges. Not thinking about her lush mouth and—

"Stop that," I said to myself as much as to her. "What I like doesn't matter. It's beyond foolish to plan to winter in a castle built into a waking volcano, whether you believe a hibernating dragon in the bowels of it is the cause or not. You've heard the stories from Nahanau—"

She cut me off with a toss of her glossy red-gold curls. When she'd worn her hair long, it had tumbled in waves around her slender dancer's body, like silk made fire. Since she'd cut it to escape her Tala abductor—another scenario I revisited compulsively as continually checking a bad tooth—it bounced in perfect ringlets. Even knowing that it was her particular magic to be beautiful no matter what, I found myself continually astounded by it. She regularly reassured me that her hair would grow long again, remembering how I'd loved to fist my hands in the spectacular length and believing I missed it. She was right that I did miss it, but wrong that I minded. I loved her with hopeless and aching finality, no matter what the details. Even when she was being an obstinate idiot. As she was at the moment.

"Maybe Glorianna wants us to liberate the Windroven dragon, too."

I ground my teeth, the old scar tissue in my jaw aching with it. Ami liked to pull out the goddess's will to reinforce her arguments—a sometimes amusing, often annoying foible of hers. The problem was, the poetic description of Ami as Glorianna's avatar might well be more than fancy. The goddess did seem to favor her, possibly to the point of speaking through her.

"You are playing games with Stella and Astar's lives, too," I finally said, my ultimate gambit to get her to listen to reason.

Her eyes flashed from twilight blue to cobalt. Even the goddess of love has her merciless aspect. "You don't have to come if you're afraid. Don't let me keep you from important business elsewhere."

And there we were. At one of many possible scenarios I'd imagined. Ami was finally dismissing me.

"Do you want me to go?" I asked carefully, keeping the frustrated rage and disappointment out of my voice. It still croaked badly, as it had ever since I burned away the brand that marked me a convict. I'd thought I'd braced myself against this eventuality, but judging by the sudden ache in my heart, I'd been sadly mistaken.

Ami bit her lip, fair face whiter than the snowflakes swirling around it. "Is that what you want?"

"What I want doesn't matter, Your Highness. It's up to you to keep or dismiss me."

"Stop talking like that," she snapped.

"Like what?" I returned, taking time to compose myself before meeting her gaze evenly.

"Oh!" She half-snarled, half-screeched it, her high cheekbones graced with a pink flush of emotion now. "Enough with that inscrutable White Monk attitude. You'd drive Glorianna Herself to slap you."

"It's not an attitude. I *am* one of the White Monks." A fact I'd been sharply reminded of when the father of my order arrived at Ordnung to crown our new High Queen in the name of Glorianna. As with all monks of my order, he'd taken—and kept—a vow of silence, and yet made it clear that he wouldn't censure me for breaking my own vow. Or rather, that I'd shattered it, completely unable to resist speaking to Ami. She is ever the one who makes me abandon all resolve.

The father had let me know I'd be welcome to return to the brotherhood and renew my vow at any time. I'd always nursed the idea in the back of my mind that when Ami tired of me, maybe I'd go back there. Knowing they would have me lit a feeble candle in the well of darkness that would be life without Ami. Perhaps I could once again find solace in silence. Not speaking had worked before, had helped me circumscribe the wanting, the endless yearning for things I didn't deserve and could never have.

"Is that what this is about?" Ami asked, voice chill. "You're wanting to return to the order. Or you want to go back to Annfwn. I know living there was your dream and you only left it because of me. I might point out that I never asked you to. You left because Andi asked it of you, and you obeyed because you're loyal to her."

"Andromeda is Queen of the Tala, my people." My adopted people. The Tala hadn't exactly embraced my presence in Annfwn, but at least there I wasn't branded a criminal. "Of course I follow her commands. And good thing, too—was I supposed to let you die in childbirth?" Ami had nearly bled out before I reached her. Another set of nightmare images I'd never shake.

"I'm grateful, naturally." She stared steadily ahead now, her jaw tight, pressing her lips together like she did when she tried not to weep. I steeled myself against offering comfort. She wouldn't want it, not from the man who distressed her in the first place. "But I can see that it's been unfair of me to keep you with me for so long. I know I'm selfish, and I forget to pay attention to what other people want and need, but I've been trying to be a better person."

I groaned to myself and concentrated on prying Astar's chubby fingers out of my horse's mane. The little brat had all of his mother's tenacity. "You're not selfish, Ami. I came to you of my own free will. And then you needed me to get Stella back. I *offered* to help you."

"I know." Her usually musical voice sounded small, and she scrubbed tears off her cheeks, just like Stella during one of her rages. "But I should have released you before this. Once we got the twins back safely, I should have told you to go."

She shouldn't have needed to tell me. I should have left sooner. As soon as we recovered Stella. But I hadn't been able to make myself go. Would it have been easier then? I'd been braced for it, but then one thing had led to the next, and she hadn't sent me away. I'd maybe begun to nurse a spot of hope that she never would, despite practicing daily for this moment.

"I'm sorry," I told her, though for my pain or her distress, I wasn't sure. "I should have gone then."

She nodded, sniffling. "It would have been better." Her voice caught on a little sob and Stella caught a whiff of her misery—a miracle it had taken that long—looked up at her, wrinkling her face in a mirror of her mother's, the toddler's tears welling up, too.

"Don't cry, Mommy!"

Astar looked over and his own face crumpled, not out of the same magically fueled empathy as Stella's, but through the nearly as magical connection to his twin. He sent up a wail, reaching so suddenly for his mother that I barely caught him before he tumbled from the saddle. Fortunately, though I couldn't shapeshift—far too late for me to learn, if I ever even could have—I possessed enough shapeshifter speed to match his. His cries turned furious, and he fought my grip, turning into a black bear cub, raking my wrists and hands with his claws. I hissed at the sting, red blood running as if from the wound in my heart.

Stella, not to be outdone, screeched like an owl. Driven by her mother's emotions, which she felt but couldn't understand, she became a golden-furred mountain lion cub and leapt from the saddle, bounding off into the snow. Astar tried to follow, growing ever more furious at being restrained.

"Let him go." Ami threw up her hands. "We won't get them settled again until they've blown off some steam."

I did as commanded, letting Astar run off after his sister. Their Tala nurses, who'd been flying above in bird form, darted after them, keeping them in sight. Ami watched them go, her face determinedly averted.

"Let's move off the road," I said. "Might as well take a break."

She nodded. "I'll bind up your scratches for you."

"Thank you," I answered, knowing I sounded stiff. Better, though, than asking how she planned to bandage my mortally wounded heart.

~ 2 ~

"**I** NEVER INTENDED to cause you pain, Ami," I told the top of her head as she worked to clean the cuts. Brutally insufficient words to describe the depth of what I'd never intended. Beginning with laying a finger on her royal, unblemished skin. Even with her tending me out of simple sympathy, in broad view of the travelers on the main highway, the least brush of her fingers on my skin brought up the insatiable lust for her, hard and hot.

She looked up at me and creaked out a smile through still damp eyes. "I know that. And you've made me so happy." She took a deep breath. "I always understood, though, that this was temporary."

"We both understood that, from the first night by the lake."

Her smile went tremulous. "When I seduced you, despite your better judgement."

I laughed, though it never comes out right. It always sounds more like a groan scraping out of my scarred throat. "Everything with you has been against my better judgement, Ami. And I've never been able to help myself. You burn so bright."

"Like staring into the sun," she said, an oddly sorrowful crease at the corners of her eyes. Her innate magic made her beautiful even in tears and other extremes of emotion—and my passionate queen ranged through many extremes—so rarely did she look as she did now, smudged with unhappiness, dented by my careless handling of her. "Do you remember when you said that to me? You said you were afraid you'd come away burned and blinded."

"I remember," I allowed. I did so much better with silence. I should never have broken my vow. If I hadn't, we wouldn't have come to this pass.

"You said that if you stared into the sun too long, you'd be immolated, and the only freedom for you would be to stay far, far away."

Never mistake that a mind sharp as a sword lies behind that pretty face. She likely remembered every word I'd ever said to her, both the wise and the incautious.

"When we said goodbye back then," she continued softly, giving me a sharp look to point out that she noticed I hadn't replied, "I thought I would never see you again."

I found my voice to answer. "I thought so, too."

"There, all better." She patted the bandages and stepped back. I flexed my fingers, as if checking the tightness, but truly to keep myself from reaching for her, from dragging her against me and begging her to let me stay forever. "When you first said that to me," she continued, "I told you not to look. If you don't look at the sun, you won't be burned and blinded. Remember?"

I nodded, remembering everything about that night with crystalline clarity. The moment she offered herself to me, she who'd always been as far beyond my reach as Glorianna Herself, all that is both softly and fiercely bright in the world.

I'd been in prison when I heard the first bard sing her praises. They'd thought to soothe us savage beasts with pretty songs. Unwise musician, however, to instill in us images of a nubile young maiden, beautiful beyond mortal comprehension. Not what you offer the hearts and minds of men little better than animals. They'd thought the minstrel well-protected, set above and apart from the mass of crippled shapeshifters and mossback criminals.

Always underestimating the depths to which men can sink. Those who only appear to be men, anyway.

I'd held back—not because I exercised more self-discipline than the others. As a boy of only fifteen who'd never so much as held a girl's hand, I'd been a seething, feral mass of longing. I hadn't even been sure *what* I wanted, only that the dark needs drove me beyond rational thought. Along with the others, I'd lunged for the source of the fantasy, but I'd been too scrawny, too weak compared to the rest, trampled and pushed to the back.

One of many stories I'd never told Ami.

Remembering, I flexed my hands again, surprised to see them clean and bandaged, rather than covered in blood. Impossible that I'd come from that and now shared a bed with the object of my obsessive and tainted lust. Though I tried to resist her, I never could. And that inability brought me to her bed, time and again.

And every bruise I left on her fair flesh in my coarse impatience felt like yet another scar on my twisted soul.

"Ash—where did you go?" Ami asked softly, and I focused on her face.

"I was remembering," I said, hoarse with need and self-loathing.

"I don't regret that night," she said. "Or anything since, but I think I was wrong to say that to you. It was never a permanent solution."

"It wasn't?" I wanted so badly to touch her, to at least hold her one last time. The Tala nurses emerged from the woods, back in human form and carrying the twins, still in their animal shapes but apparently more docile.

Ami shook her head, hair catching the light like living flame. "I've really tried to give up feeling sorry for myself, as I know I'm blessed and should be grateful, but sometimes this beauty feels more like a curse, like people only see the pretty exterior and don't see *me*." She glared at me, defying me to argue with her.

I didn't know what to say, so I said nothing and she huffed out an exasperated sound.

"The point is, Ash, that it's not enough for you to close your eyes. I need *you* to see me."

"I see you," I replied, my whisper harsh as the ravens calling in the trees.

Her face crumpled a little and she looked down, worrying her fingers together, pale with chill as she'd taken off her gloves to tend me. "Do you? Sometimes I don't think you do. I know it's… difficult for you to be with me, even though you love me."

"I do love you, Amelia. I love you more than my own life."

She glanced up at me again, her face wet with renewed tears, and she smiled through them. "I know you do. And I love you—but it's not enough, is it? I know you're not happy."

"Maybe I'm just not a happy person," I offered.

"Is that all?" She searched my face. "Be honest with me, because I know there's a lot of stuff that goes on in your head that you don't share with me and that's fine—" She held up a hand when I tried to speak, then pulled her gloves from her pocket and yanked them on. "Really, I'm fine with that. I've reconciled myself to it because if you wanted to let me in, you would. The thing is, you clearly don't want to. For a while I thought, well that will change, but it hasn't. If anything, you're more closed off than ever. And… this isn't enough for me anymore. Ironically enough, *you* were the one to open my eyes and make me want more than the fairytale. My marriage with Hugh was a lovely fantasy, and maybe if he'd lived, we would have found something real there once the shine wore off. All I know is that I loved him, and I love you, but love doesn't solve everything. It doesn't make us good for each other." She wiped her face and pulled up the hood of her cloak, taking refuge in the deep cowl.

No, I wasn't good for her. And love was never enough. It hadn't been enough to save my parents. They'd loved each other, and so my father had stopped looking for Annfwn, and stayed with her, they'd had a baby and raised me together. Then the priests had come for him and burned him at the stake for being a shapeshifting demon. At thirteen, I'd gone to prison. And my mother had died, alone and undefended.

Love never saved anyone, and it couldn't make me into someone I wasn't.

"You're right," I told her. "It's time for us to say goodbye." It came out well enough. Glorianna knew I'd practiced the line enough times.

"I think so," Ami finally said. When she faced me again, she'd composed herself and stopped actively weeping, though her eyes seemed even larger and bluer with the glow of unshed tears. "Delaying this has only brought us both pain."

I nodded slowly. For once we understood each other perfectly well.

Our entourage was reassembling, the Tala nurses back in human form and taking the twins into the carriage, hopefully to coax them into a nap. Ami followed the direction of my gaze. "Maybe I'll go ride with the kids."

"All right. I'll take care of your horse."

She took a step. Turned back. "Are you—are you leaving now?"

It would be easier. Though I'd have to choose—through the mountains to Annfwn or east, to the temple of the White Monks. Neither held appeal. I also had a responsibility to fulfill. I might be prison scum who'd battered the heart of the only woman—maybe the only person—I'd ever loved, but I wouldn't take a chance on her safety just to make things easier on myself.

I cleared my throat. "No. I'll see you safely to Windroven." I tried for a smile. "Since you're so determined to go." Odd where this argument had begun and how it exploded from there. But then, this moment had been inevitable all along. All those problems between us we'd ignored, drowning them in kisses while they grew in the shadows we shoved them into. Showed how nicely fermented shit can make the smallest seeds grow into an impenetrable hedge of thorns, slicing you no matter how you tried to extract yourself.

Ami didn't smile back. Instead she simply nodded. Then walked away.

~ 3 ~

ECHOING THE BLACKNESS of my mood, the clouds drew in dark and forbidding by late afternoon, a biting wind whipping up to slap my face. Much as Ami had wanted to do. Upon reflection, I wished she had. The chill formality of our fight hadn't been like either of us. Better if she had raged at me.

But perhaps it made sense. Always we'd been easiest with each other when flush with passion, caught up and not overthinking anything—whether it was sex or the battle to save Stella. Perhaps an affair born in fire inevitably died in the grip of ice.

Ami had stayed in the carriage all day, making me wonder how they kept the twins occupied. Sleeping, most likely, which boded ill for any inn we stayed at. And we *would* have to stop for the night. The impending storm and our slow progress demanded it. Even if we pressed on, we wouldn't make Windroven before the early hours before dawn at our current rate.

"By the look of those clouds, we should be looking for a place to stay the night," Lieutenant Graves remarked, pulling his steed up behind mine. He nodded unnecessarily at the storm building on the southwest horizon, obviously steaming in our direction. "Those aren't Mornai clouds to my eye, but that'll be a decent enough blow that we don't want to be caught out in it, if you want this Avonlidgh farmboy's opinion, sir."

I glanced at him wryly for the *sir*, and for his diffidence. Graves and his men had served Amelia from the beginning, at her father-in-law's behest, and they all knew exactly who I was. Graves had probably recognized it in me even before he saw the scarring from the prison lash, long before Ami ever knew the truth about me. Why he hadn't called me on it back then—or reported my escaped prisoner status to anyone—I didn't know. I'd appreciated the courtesy, as well as getting to keep my head attached to my neck. And now with the High Queen granting pardons for Tala prisoners, I didn't have to worry about that aspect anymore. Still, calling me "sir" went a step too far.

But then Graves and his men were so intimately involved in their queen's protection and in her daily life that there were some things they couldn't pretend not to see. Ami and I had never been good at keeping our hands off each other, even when we tried to maintain proper decorum. I'd muddied the waters considerably for these good men, who'd shown me the greatest kindness by not turning me in, by allowing me to linger in their mistress's presence with such unclear status. They deferred to me as they would a prince, an affront to them as men of honor.

Yes, I'd let this go on far too long, steeped in dithering and inaction.

"There's a good inn up ahead that we stayed at before," Graves continued after a pause, making me realize I'd failed to answer. The habits of silence ran deep. "But with Willy and Nilly, I don't know…"

"Definitely not a good idea," I agreed, smiling a bit that the men had picked up on our nicknames for the twins, calling them Willy and Nilly for their reckless and unpredictable behavior. It made for a good code, too, since not everyone needed to know the location of Princess Stella and Prince Astar, heirs to three thrones and counting, including the High Throne of the Thirteen Kingdoms. Traveling with Ami, however, made all such precautions moot. She was unmistakable under any circumstances, her face better known than the High Queen's, thanks to all the artists who vied to make their fame with her face.

"I don't like going to an inn, either," I continued. "Though the Thirteen are slowly learning not to hate shapeshifters on sight, the more rural we go, the more likely we are to encounter old prejudices, I'd think."

I posed it as a question, and Graves nodded. "Ayup. There's knowing your prince and heir to the Avonlidgh throne has shapeshifter blood, and there's seeing him tearing up the curtains as a black bear cub, breaking everything in sight looking for sweets."

We shared a grin for that—as that very thing had happened more than once—and it helped lighten my morose mood. "Other suggestions?" I asked.

Graves squinched an eye at the clouds, pursing his mouth. "Her Highness has stopped on other occasions at the Duchess of Lianore's manse. She's a good lady and loyal. Tolerant," he added with a grimace.

"All right," I agreed, "I'll speak to the queen about it."

He saluted—which he shouldn't, but it would have been churlish to say so. Removing myself from this equation would solve a great deal for everyone. I guided my steed alongside the carriage, rapping the back of my knuckles on the window frame.

The curtains whisked open and Ami glared at me, then set her expression in impassive lines. When she spoke, she used regal tones. "What do you need?"

She'd been weeping—again or still—her eyes uncharacteristically puffy with it. When I'd first met her, she'd been paralyzed with grief for Hugh and hadn't been able to cry. I supposed it said something that she was able to shed tears for our imminent parting. Better and healthier for her. No reason the sight should make me angry.

"Graves suggests that we ask the Duchess of Lianore to let us stay the night, Your Highness," I told her, submerging the anger under icy formality. Two could play that game. "There's a storm coming and with Willy—the twins, it would be best to avoid inns."

"Lady Veronica?" She brightened a little. "An excellent idea. I'd love to see her."

"All right, I'll send ahead to let her know of our arrival."

"Fine," she replied. Then raised her brows. "Anything else?"

I looked past her to Stella, asleep with her two smallest fingers in her mouth, draped over her mother's lap. I couldn't see Astar, but the lack of ruckus indicated he was also sleeping. "We'll never get them to sleep tonight if you let them nap all day."

It was the wrong thing to say. One of many reasons I took refuge in saying nothing. Ami's cheeks flushed and her eyes flashed almost luminescent, like the toxic violet gases in the marshes of Biah. "That strikes me as something that is not your problem," she answered, voice colder and more biting than the wind that tried to snatch at my cloak.

I blew out a breath. "Ami, I only meant—"

"I don't care what you meant." She rubbed her eyes and looked away. "I'm tired and I'm willing to face a long night for a few hours of peace right now, all right? It's not like I'll be doing anything else with my time. At least I won't be distracted by you."

I stiffened at the well-aimed jab. Finding time alone together had become a challenge, even with the Tala nurses and other retainers. The twins loved being with their mother best, especially Stella, who seemed to understand she'd been unfairly deprived of Ami's loving care for that first month she'd been in her abductor's hands and was determined to make up for it. If they couldn't have Ami, they wanted to be climbing on me, showering me with affection that warmed even the burned-out coal of my heart. It struck me then that I'd be losing Astar and Stella, too, when I left.

They would be too young to remember me. Much better for them, as they shouldn't be warped by my presence, seeing a man like me as some sort of father figure. A bitter comfort.

Still, I'd thought Ami enjoyed the sneaking about, finding places to be together where we wouldn't be discovered. Especially when I put my hand over her mouth to muffle her cries of pleasure, and sternly ordered her not to move. All for discretion's sake—but also a game that excited us both. The memories of those stolen moments sent a shudder of need through me, and I wanted her with as much helpless lust as ever. The thought of never touching her again…

"Ash," she whispered, her eyes dark on my face before she determinedly averted them. "Don't look at me that way. I … can't."

I nodded stiffly and tried to think of what I should say.

"Would you—" She held up a hand alongside her face, as if shielding her eyes from the sun. "Would you please just go away?"

I nodded again, even though she wouldn't see it, and rode into the wind to tell Graves of the decision.

~ 4 ~

"YOUR HIGHNESS, QUEEN Amelia—welcome to Lianore!" The duchess swept a deep curtsey to Ami, her elaborate brocaded skirts glittering with crystals.

"Lady Veronica." Ami brushed self-consciously at her skirts, then held out her hands to raise up the older woman. I knew Ami felt underdressed in her traveling gown and cloak. Never mind that she outshone everyone, even dressed in peasant rags. Another aspect of how she lacked the confidence others assumed she possessed—she liked to be polished or she felt vulnerable. "It's so good of you to welcome us with no notice."

"Not good of me at all, Your Highness," Lady Veronica assured her. "This manse is enormous and benefits from having people stay. And, I've a number of parties planned for the Feast of Moranu—your blessing on the preparations will guarantee that I'm the most popular hostess of the season! Also, I'll be able to make everyone jealous that I've seen the precious prince and princess." She peeked ostentatiously around Ami to Willy and Nilly—thankfully in human form, but hiding behind their mother's full skirts—then curtseyed again. "Welcome to Lianore, Your Highnesses. Princess Stella, Prince Astar—do you like pastries and sugared fruits?"

Wonderful. No way the twins would pass up that offer and

impossible that they'd sleep any time soon. Ami glanced over her shoulder at me, gaze opaque, a set to her mouth that dared me to comment. I kept quiet. She'd told me it wasn't my problem.

Astar hung back still, but Stella pushed forward—small fingers in her mouth, but beaming—and nodded emphatically. Following her lead, and not one to miss out on a treat of any sort, Astar stepped out, threw back his head and howled, but fortunately retained human shape.

The duchess gestured the children toward the feast hall—an invitation they accepted by taking off at top speed—and Ami looped her arm through Lady Veronica's, her bright head tilted toward the darker one.

Servants stepped up to show us men the way to the barracks, though Graves knew the way. I followed along, habitually checking the security of the premises. The Duchess of Lianore had been widowed a number of years and had preserved her lands and manse intact despite several internecine conflicts. She was no fool—and the alertness of her guards reflected that.

"Lord Ash!" the duchess called.

I looked back to see her hastening after me. "Come and join us." She smiled warmly and I automatically took the hands she held out, her fingers thin and festooned with rings. Large earrings with cascades of crystals matching those on her gown sparkled with the chagrined shake of her head. "So rude of me," she said in a conspiratorial whisper, "not to make sure you knew to come with us, not go with the men at arms." She looped her arm through mine, giving me a choice between going with her or fighting her off. "But you'll forgive me, won't you? I'm sure you know better than most how dazzling your lady can be."

"Thank you, Your Grace," I tried, "but I am no lord and—"

"Nonsense. I'll make you a lord of one of my little properties if I must. It's hardly a secret, the *amour* you share with our lovely queen." She winked at me. "You make her happy, so you at least deserve a small farm and cottage. I shall dub you Lord Sousbois. It's a small place, but I doubt you'll spend any time there."

Though a bright star of a headache formed behind the bridge of my nose, I could no more argue with her and still be polite than I could resist her elegantly dragging me into the feast hall. The long table for dining guests was set as if a party might commence at any moment—and grander than anything I'd ever seen, even at Castle Avonlidgh. Old King Erich, Hugh's father, had been an ancient warhorse of a soldier, a relic of the Great War, and treated the capital of Avonlidgh more as a fortress than anything. I understood why Ami found the place gloomy in its austerity. And Castle Ordnung, despite best efforts to restore it to something of its former glory, still couldn't match this—even if Her Majesty had been the sort to have the patience for it.

My parents had celebrated the Feast of Moranu when I was young, but had never possessed the wherewithal for anything on this scale. Still, I recognized many of the elements. The impoverished boy in me soaked it in with delighted wonder—and a bite of jealousy at what he'd missed. That same poisonous envy that had plagued me watching all those men dance with Ami.

In keeping with the goddess's rule over shadows and the dark of night, the table had been draped entirely in black silk, but with silver threads woven in that caught the candlelight. Crystal plates and goblets sparkled with fire, and the cutlery looked to be entirely silver. White gems of all shapes and sizes were scattered over the cloth, like thousands of stars, and a garland of white moonflowers gleamed like sweetly scented, living pearls all down the center.

A golden light radiated from black candles set in elaborate

crystal candelabras, both on the table and suspended from the high ceiling by silver wires. Moonflower garlands dripping with flashing crystals—and possibly diamonds—festooned the walls, windows, mantels, and every other possible surface. It reminded me of Annfwn, in all her tropical beauty, but rendered in the colors of winter.

"It's extravagant, I know," Veronica said, squeezing my arm and giving a happy sigh, "but the Feast of Moranu has always been my favorite, since I was a little girl. I'm happy to have the little prince and princess see it."

Ami and the children had gathered at one end of the hall, beneath a living tree blooming with more moonflowers. Blown glass and crystal ornaments dangled from the branches. Astar eyed them with feline interest. He'd recently discovered a black cat form and liked it entirely too much for climbing to satisfy his curiosity. Ami sat on the black fur mounded around the base of the tree, her skirts spread around her and a plate of goodies on her lap. Stella had her own plate and had already smeared her face with something bright pink. Ami held out another, similar tidbit, trying to tempt Astar back.

"Astar, darling," she cooed, though I clearly heard the edge of aggravation beneath her dulcet tone. "Look at this, Astar."

He twitched, eyes fixed on a chain of glass balls. I knew the moment he decided to go for it—maybe by the flexing of his chubby knees or simply knowing the boy well—and he leapt into the air, flashing into the black kitten form in the same movement. Forewarned, I'd already slipped the duchess's arm and used shapeshifter speed to nab him in midair. He hissed and spit, but fortunately his claws in that form weren't nearly as formidable as the bear cub.

"Bad Willy cat," I told him, tapping him on the tender nose.

"No."

"Aww, give him here." The duchess held out her arms.

"He scratches," I warned her.

"I have cats," she replied, capturing him securely. "Real ones," she added, "but I know how to handle an ornery kitty. They all think they're royalty, shapeshifting prince or no. C'mon love, how about some fresh cream? Or I have kippers."

He mewled, rubbing his whiskers on her chin, the traitorous brat. Stella tumbled her plate off her lap—and onto her mother—became a kitten, too, and chased after both of them. With a groan of exasperation, Ami began plucking up the spilled sweetmeats—to the horror of a maidservant who ran over, crying that Her Highness mustn't and then tying herself up trying to curtsey, intervene, and apologize all at the same time.

"Your Highness," I said to Ami and held out a hand, "allow me to assist you and we can make room for the maids to do their job."

She let me help her up, though she hardly needed it with her lithe dancer's grace, and she scowled at the bright pink whatever-it-was now smeared down the bodice of her travelling gown.

"Oh, Your Highness!" exclaimed another maid, as horrified as if Ami were bleeding from a mortal wound. "I'm so sorry!" She cast anxious glances at the duchess, who happily entertained the two kitties with what looked like a basket of yarn. Despite the lady's affection for felines, judging by the clockwork perfection of her house, the duchess likely did not tolerate poor performance by her staff.

"Your Highness wanted to change after a long day of travel, didn't you?" I inserted. "I'll escort you to your rooms. The duchess has the prince and princess well in hand and I'm sure your trunks have arrived by now." I bowed to Ami, and gestured for her to precede me. I'd thought to spare her—or myself—the moment that she'd refuse my arm, but she gave me such a furiously injured glare that I realized it had been a miscalculation.

Nevertheless, she swept past me, leaving simmering scorn and the scent of roses in her wake. A footman fortunately appeared to guide her, and I followed behind at a respectful distance. I would have discreetly lost myself along the way, but I needed to check her chambers to be sure all was safe before I turned over that responsibility to the Lianore guards. Once inside, a group of ladies—Ami's personal maid and some from Lianore—enveloped her, whisking her off. I made a circuit of the richly appointed chambers, checking the windows where thick snow swirled outside in the night, and returned to the drawing room via a side entrance, thinking to slip out the door.

Only to find Ami standing in front of it, still in her stained dress, alone, spine rigid and chin regally lifted. All the maids and other ladies had been sent away. She folded her arms, which deepened her creamy cleavage, and I forced my gaze to the door behind her, staring at it instead. Longingly.

"Did Your Highness need something else?" I inquired when she didn't say anything.

"Oh, stop it!" she snapped, her cheeks high with color.

"Stop what?" I asked cautiously. Probably a good thing my Ami couldn't shift into anything with claws. By the look of her, I'd have been eviscerated long since.

"Stop 'your highnessing' me to death. Being all polite. You're not fooling anyone. And if you think you're escaping, you're not. You might as well stay because Veronica thinks we're happy lovers, a cozy little family, and figured on all four of us sharing these rooms tonight." She pointed her slim nose at me, daring me to complain.

"I thought you said that—"

"I know what I said. And I've changed my mind. The Tala nurses took off to shift and sleep outside—you know how they are. I'm exhausted and I'm going to bed. *You* can stay up with Willy and Nilly, since you're so determined to be done with us."

I regarded her cautiously, trying to parse her logic. "That makes no sense."

She firmed her lips and looked away, her rigidity collapsing. "I don't care. And I don't want to fight with you again. Can we just… not?" The wretched expression in her eyes undid me and I stepped toward her before I came to my senses and remembered I was the one who put the misery there. Instead, I put my hands inside the flowing sleeves of my coat, grasping the opposite wrists, an old habit from wearing monk's robes.

"I'm sorry, Ami," I said quietly, which seemed to be the only thing I could think of to say to her.

"Me too." Her voice came out small and she hiccoughed a little. "I really hate this, you know?"

"I know. Me too." I offered her a lopsided smile and she returned it, tremulously. "Go to bed," I told her. "Get some rest. I'll round up Willy and Nilly and keep them out of trouble."

"Are you sure?" She looked both hopeful and terribly sad. "They're not your responsibility. They never have been and you've always been so good about it. Good to them and me. And I'm just horrible."

"You're not horrible, Ami." I bit back telling her I loved her. She knew that and it didn't help any of this. "And I'm sure. Get some sleep and things will look better in the morning. I've got this handled."

"You always do." I couldn't interpret the twist she put on that. She bit her lip, as if wishing she could take it back, then burst out, "But don't let them fall asleep in cat form. It's not good for them and—"

"Ami," I interrupted, "I know."

"They're so young," she explained, eyes filling with tears again. "And I can't stop crying."

"It's been a long day. A hard one after a long night. You need to sleep."

She wiped her nose and nodded, then turned and held up her shoulder-length hair from her high collar. "Would you undo my laces? I can't deal with the maids right now."

"Of course," I said, though I had to clear my throat to get it out. How many times had I performed this simple service for her? Hundreds, in just the short time we'd known each other. The cloth parted, revealing her sugary skin, the sweet curve of her spine all the way down to the most perfect ass created by Glorianna. My fingers burned to caress those lines. So many times we'd initiated sex this way—me loosening the laces and revealing her glorious body as I stripped her naked. If I'd realized, the last time I did this, that I'd never again have the privilege, I might have lingered over it. Instead we'd gone at it in a furious rush, both of us too impatient to savor.

As we'd done everything between us.

My hands shook, so I tucked them in my sleeves again. "There." My voice grated over gravel, barely audible. She glanced over her shoulder at me, clutching the loosened dress to her bosom, eyes wide and full of emotion. The same thoughts had occurred to her, I felt sure, and I wondered if she felt the same regret.

"Ash…" she said, but didn't finish.

"Go to bed, Ami," I told her again. "I'll handle things."

She dipped her chin, lashes fluttering against her cheeks, then turned away and went into the bedroom, closing the door firmly behind her.

~ 5 ~

THE NEXT MORNING dawned bright and clear, fortunately. I was gritty-eyed enough from lack of sleep that I wouldn't have wanted to face talking Ami out of traveling through a blizzard. I'd played with the kittens awhile, then coaxed them into playing I Eat You, a game the shapeshifter kids in Annfwn loved to play. That had them trying several different forms, which—along with a well-timed sugar crash—wore them out enough to fall asleep sometime before dawn.

At least they'd be easy to load up, as they were still fast asleep. The Tala nurses reappeared at daybreak and bundled up the kids, laughing merrily when I grumped at them for their defection the night before. Tala are notoriously difficult to intimidate. We might as well have cats as nurses.

Ami, looking as fresh and gorgeous as the sunrise in a white gown decorated with gold stars, chatted happily with the duchess, saying her farewells, while I conferred with Graves on our route. The duchess had loaned Ami several white and gold open sleighs in lieu of our carriages, which would not only enable us to travel much faster over the freshly fallen snow, but also to cut across the countryside and make directly for Windroven, rather than sticking to the more roundabout roads. When the twins awoke, they should at least be entertained enough by the novelty of the transportation to stay out of trouble.

What we'd find when we reached Windroven was another story.

"But, Your Highness, it can't be safe," the duchess was saying to Ami, who smiled indulgently. "The stories I've been hearing… And some of them from my own people, who I trust implicitly. Stay here for the Feast of Moranu. There's plenty of room and I'm delighted to have you."

"If only because it will make you the most envied hostess in the Thirteen," Ami teased with a brilliant smile.

Lady Veronica toyed with one of her earrings, assuming a demure expression. "Well, a girl can't avoid such consequences." Then she sobered. "But I'm very serious, Your Highness. Stay here. Don't go to Windroven. Not with the volcano making those noises and a succession of Mornai storms predicted." She spotted me and beckoned me over peremptorily. "Ash, tell her. Her Highness will listen to you."

Ami gazed at me expectantly, blue eyes clear as the sky framed by the sunrise of her hair, full mouth curved in regal serenity. She'd recovered all her poise—and had once again erected a wall of impermeable ice between us. I bowed to her formally, largely to acknowledge the distance she'd reestablished. Better this way.

"I have advised Her Highness as much, Your Grace, but she is determined."

"I am," Ami inserted, smiling at the duchess to soften the declaration. "Hugh's people have told me that volcano has rumbled off and on for generations. If it didn't, it wouldn't be alive to keep us warm through the winter."

"Well, and indeed that's true, Your Highness, but never like this. And with the magic returned to the world, well, you know what they say." She glanced about and leaned in. "The *dragon*," she whispered loudly.

"I've dealt with more cantankerous creatures than dragons," Ami informed her airily, sliding a hard-eyed look at me, so I wouldn't mistake her meaning. "They're easy to chase off, despite their growling. Cowards at heart."

The duchess, far too refined to reveal if she understood the undercurrents, simply waved her hand as yet another sleigh pulling up, drawn by more horses from her stables. "If I cannot dissuade Your Highness, I can at least send along decorations and supplies. Glorianna only knows what a musty mess Windroven is. Sadly, the moonflowers can't withstand the cold, so I'm sending silk ones—and directions for sewing more so your maids can do that, in case they don't know how. You must at least have the traditional treats and wines for the Feast." She frowned at the sleigh as if it had failed her in some terrible fashion. "Oh, I hate to think of our queen having such a tatty Feast of Moranu. Give me another hour and I'll—"

"Thank you, Veronica, for everything." Ami embraced the duchess, cutting her off, then strolled toward the sleighs, calling out a question to Graves. Her skirts and trailing cloak left a wide swath of cleared snow behind her, punctuated by the steps of her little boots.

I stared at the trail, my attention caught. Or perhaps it was the lack of sleep catching up with me, because I shook my head to clear it of the trance when the duchess put her hand on my arm.

"It's not easy," she murmured to me, "to love a woman of higher station."

"Your Grace, I—"

"You know exactly what I mean." She raised her brows, stern as any teacher. "Nor is it easy for a woman of station to love a man of lower rank. I should know. It's a delicate balance. Especially with a man who is a true leader." Squeezing my upper arm, she made an appreciative moue, eyes sparkling with mischief. "We like our men strong and manly, as much as the next woman, or more. Dominant in the bedroom," she murmured meaningfully, and I seriously hoped she hadn't made me blush. "I know how it is. I'm not so old that I don't enjoy much the same." She nodded knowingly, her gaze straying to a large man in her personal guard, Dasnarian by his bulk and coloring. The duchess put gloved fingers under my chin, turning me to face her again. "Never think it's easy for her, to balance that."

I searched for an appropriate reply and came up empty. The honest truth about Ami was something I'd never betray by speaking aloud. I knew better than perhaps anyone all the opposing forces Ami juggled behind her frivolous exterior. I understood very well how much she struggled to be strong and confident, to compensate for the holes inside left by a mother who perished shortly after giving birth to her, sisters who left her behind, and a husband who died far too young. People looked at her and saw Queen Amelia of Avonlidgh, avatar of Glorianna, and the most beautiful woman alive.

Ami said I didn't see her, but I did. I knew her heart better than my own. Which meant I understood full well how difficult our love affair made everything for her.

She'd called herself selfish, but that flaw belonged to me. I'd only added to her troubles, wanting to eke out more time with her, when I would have helped her most by absenting myself from the complications of her life.

Ami needed to move on, to consolidate her position as

queen, to find her way as a mother, to think about who her king should be. Maybe even some time just to be herself, not to worry about who she danced with or how to balance her loves with her responsibilities. She deserved a man who could be a real husband to her, who could help her rule.

One that her nobles like the Duchess of Lianore wouldn't have to resort to subterfuges of false titles to accommodate.

I bowed deeply to the duchess, thanking her for her advice—and for her concern.

"We love our queen," she told me with the fervency of absolute honesty. "Take care of her for us. Promise me, Lord Sousbois."

I promised I would, not caring for the bitter taste of the lie.

THE REST OF the journey to Windroven went extraordinarily quickly—so much so that I'd have believed Ami's claim that Glorianna smoothed our way. One of many phenomena that made me think she might truly be Glorianna's avatar. Both the woman and the goddess liked to arrange things to suit themselves.

And both seemed to relish their hold on me. Most Tala, even part-bloods, look to Moranu, the goddess of trickery and mutability. But from my earliest days, even before I took my vow to the White Monks, formally consecrating myself to Glorianna, I'd felt the hand of the goddess of morning. My mother had been devout in Glorianna's worship, as most good country girls were, and I'd put down my own devotion to the goddess as early childhood indoctrination.

With the path my life had followed since… It might be better to say that Glorianna had wrapped one fist around my heart and the other around my cock—merrily leading me by both.

As if she heard the irreverent thought, Ami turned to look at me then, her eyes so blue they pierced me even from a distance. She crooked a finger at me, a slight smile on her face, enjoying playing with me. Because I, of course, hastened immediately to her side.

"We're here just in time," she said, gesturing at the mountain climbing against the darkening sky. "Another storm is coming in off the ocean."

I squinted at the clouds wreathing the turrets of the castle and highest crags of the sleeping volcano. Though I didn't need to. I'd been watching the storm approach since it first darkened the horizon, like a rippling banner showing where Windroven lay. Some long-ago Avonlidgh royal had decided the quiescent volcanic mountain made the perfect foundation for a fortress. Castle Windroven had been built into and of the stone, so that its towers took the place of the long-gone peak of the mountain. In many places the architecture had been designed so deftly that the walls were indistinguishable from the base of igneous rock.

As a fortress, it worked beautifully. With a sheer drop to the sea at its back, the old volcano enjoyed an unparalleled vista of rich and flat farmland on all other sides. Windroven could not be approached undetected. The steep-sided peak itself defied scaling, leaving the winding road the sole access to the castle. On other occasions, the people of Avonlidgh would be lining that road to shower their queen, prince, and princess with rose petals and adulation. But most of the nearby denizens had fled for the winter, letting their farmlands sleep under the deep snows—and getting as far from the threatening volcano as possible.

Wiser than we.

"Those aren't only storm clouds," I told Ami, and pointed at the obscured turrets. "See there? That's smoke. There's a column of it rising up behind the castle. Look around you at the snow. It's gray with ash. The volcano is active."

"Rumbling only," she replied. "I'm not concerned. Glorianna will watch over us."

"Your Highness—"

"Speaking of fretting," Ami cut me off, "isn't this your opportunity to leave? No sense making the trip to the top only to go back down again." She gestured to the road that curved to meet up with us again. "In another hour's ride you could be at the inn at the crossroads. I'd hate for you to be traveling still when the snow hits."

I'd stiffened, stricken with the imminence of parting, a stinging retort ready on my tongue until that last. Ami meant it. Despite her hurt and anger, she didn't want me at risk. Her eyes told the tale, even as she firmed her trembling lips and looked away to stare at the belching mountain. Perfectly apt that the home she'd so readily adopted was both spectacular and treacherous.

"I'm safe at home, Ash," she said. "I won't keep you from your life's path any longer. It would mean a great deal to me, if—" She swallowed hard against something. More tears, maybe. But when she met my gaze, her eyes weren't damp, but hard and bright as Lianore's diamonds. "I'd like to know that you're safe, too. I know I might never hear from you again, so let me imagine that. You, warm and fed—and just at the inn down the road. Where I can pretend to myself that I could go. Take an hour's ride, and lurk in the shadows, and just…reassure myself."

"Ami," I said, my voice more broken than usual. Words as always escaped me.

"A silly fantasy. I know you won't stay there or anything."

"And you could never lurk in the shadows," I managed with a half-smile.

She laughed, a little watery, a lot brittle. The sound made me want to hold her, and I must have moved like I might dismount, because she held up a hand. "I feel like we've said goodbye so many times already. Would you do me this favor and just go. Now. Like you're off to scout ahead."

I glanced at the other sleigh, where the twins still slept with their nurses. They'd be up all night again, but I'd miss it. And I wouldn't get to say goodbye to them. Though that was likely just as well. It would only confuse and upset them.

Ami followed my line of sight, then met my gaze again. "Please."

A more articulate man would have thought of parting words. Something meaningful, for her and for me, to remember in the days ahead.

But I only nodded, bowing from the waist, and turned my horse's head toward the road leading away from Windroven.

~ *6* ~

AMI'S SCREAM RENT the air.

I knew it well—even at a distance. So well that I'd already wheeled my horse around and with one mind we leapt into a flat-out gallop before I even processed what the sound was. So many times we'd drilled this alarm system, during those days we'd traveled through the Wild Lands and into Annfwn seeking Stella. I'd taught Ami how to wield a short blade and the considerable power of her lungs, to protect herself long enough for me to get to her.

Snow flew in a blizzard of our own making as my steed and I barreled down the road at top speed. Had I the ability, I would have taken wing to get there faster. My heart pounded as if I were the one running.

I should never have left her.

We passed the fork and followed the road, though the sleigh tracks veered to cut across the fallow snow-covered fields. The mare couldn't go as fast in the soft drifts as we could on the snow-packed road, which still wasn't fast enough. In the vast open whiteness, I should be able to see…

There. So far out.

At my signal, we bounded off the road, lurching through the drifts, making for the dark spots of the line of sleighs. Other shapes darted in and out, worrying the outriders like wolves attacking a herd, trying for the vulnerable center.

Blood boiled in my ears, my thighs clamped around the horse, urging the gelding on, feeling as if I tried to lift him up through each lunge. With screaming urgency, I wanted to leap from his back and go it myself, but I knew, *knew*, I'd only go more slowly. Never had I more bitterly regretted my inability to shapeshift.

Ami had stopped screaming—I only hoped because she trusted I'd heard and was on my way, not because she couldn't—and the only sounds other than the whisk of wind over snow were the grunts of Graves and his men, fighting the silent beasts.

As I watched, still helplessly too far away, a horse and rider went down, the black-furred shapes swarming it. My own gelding and I caught the scent at the same time, the sticky sweetness of corruption, of magic-born undeath. He faltered in his great-hearted speed, wanting to balk, and I ruthlessly clamped down on his mind, forcing him to go on.

It made me as bad as those black-souled practitioners of *Deyrr* who'd surely created the attacking creatures—I knew that smell far too well from the siege at Ordnung—but in that moment I only cared about one thing. The one person I'd barter my own soul to save.

Ami. I had to get to Ami.

I caught a flash of her face, stark in the whiteness, the flame of her hair a blaze of promise that she yet lived. Then she disappeared, crouching down into the sleigh. Two of the animals fighting had to be the Tala nurses—one in wolf form, the other a big cat—worrying the attacking creatures. No sign of the twins, so hopefully Ami was sitting on them.

I plunged into the fight on the weakest side, swinging my sword to decapitate a black wolf-like creature. It went down silently, staining the snow with black ichor that had long since ceased to be blood. We'd have to go back and chop them up, then burn them, as the pieces would keep on going in their unnatural way. For the moment, disabling them was key. Graves and his men hadn't been at Ordnung, had never fought these things, and so wouldn't know that until too late.

"Chop off the heads!" I shouted to Graves. "Disable, then kill."

He nodded, the other men hearing and changing their defense. The habitual response is to stab and wound when wolves attack. Cutting off their heads takes too long with a normal creature. But these weren't natural and they never bled out, never flinched from pain. It changes the battle from one of pitting cleverness and courage against a worthy enemy to hacking apart a mindless scourge.

I took off two more heads. Shapeshifter speed lent me a certain strength and leverage the other men couldn't match. I carved my way through the pack, getting to Ami. One of the creatures climbed into the sleigh just before I got there. I went after it. I leapt off my horse and into the sled, grappling the beast, which snarled and writhed in my grip with unnatural strength.

Dropping my sword—in such close quarters, I ran too much risk of accidentally striking Ami or the kids if they got in the way of the long blade—I throttled the thing with one forearm, wrestling it back, and wishing I'd thought to draw my short blade.

"Ash!" Ami's eyes were wild blue—and far too close to the beast's slavering jaws as it snapped and lunged at her in eerie silence. To stop it, I thrust the meat of my other arm between its jaws, uncaring that it mindlessly savaged me. The pain fueled me. And better my arm than her throat. Ami, face contorted in horror, reared up, short blade fisted in both hands, and drove it into the beast's eye. A good strategy, with a normal creature. This one, of course, didn't falter.

But she gave me the blade I needed.

I let go the beast's throat, hauling it back by dint of my arm in its jaws, yanked the blade out and drove it into the spinal column at the back of its head. Black ichor sprayed my face and I pressed my lips tight against accidentally getting any of the poisonous shit in my mouth. It still mindlessly chewed, lurching to push through my restraint, and I sawed through its neck. A laborious and grim task. No speed or leverage to help me, only determination.

At last the head separated from the body, though the jaws remained locked on my arm, still gnawing away. A bright haze of shock surrounded everything with halos of light as I lifted the creature's body and threw it out of the sleigh with vehemence. It slogged through the snow, searching for prey it could no longer detect.

All of the creatures seemed to be headless now, similarly confused, and Graves and his men—along with the Tala—were working methodically to dismember them all.

"Ash!" Ami's voice grated harshly, no music in it, and she pulled the blade from my hand. "Glorianna take you, sit down before you pass out."

She began sawing at the tendons in the beast's jaw, cutting the magically animated muscles that gave it strength. Black ichor and my bright red blood fountained over her white and gold gown, no doubt ruining it forever. Ami shouldn't be covered in gore like this.

"Your dress," I managed and she threw me a ferocious glare.

"Shut up, you stupid, stupid man. I don't care about the fucking dress!" The lower jaw fell away and the head, losing its hold, dropped to the floor of the sleigh. The twins shrieked, popping tousled heads—one bright, one dark—from beneath the furry blanket where Ami had indeed been sitting on them. They screamed again when the beast's remaining eye blinked at them, the upper lip lifting over fangs in a snarl.

I grabbed it by the ear with my good hand and flung the head as far away from them as I could. For good measure, I sent the lower jaw after it. As if that sapped the last of my strength, my legs gave out, and I sat heavily.

Ami was cursing me steadily, tearing strips from her gown to bandage my arm. "If you don't die, I'm going to kill you," she muttered. Blood and ichor streaked her face, making her look like Glorianna as warrior.

"I'm all right," I told her. "Don't worry. I need to—"

"You need to shut up and sit. You've already lost too much blood."

"Are you hurt?" I tried to sit up, suddenly seized with the fear that the blood might not be all mine. "The twins?"

"*We* are fine," she bit out. "It's you who's hurt, which is thriced inconvenient since you can heal anyone but yourself. Why would you be so contrary? Just to make me crazy, I'm sure."

I watched her, bemused by her ferocity. The twins had pulled the blanket back over their heads and held on to each other. They'd have bad dreams now. So young for their first nightmares. I'd failed to save them from that.

Ami might have been right about the blood loss, because

lightning-streaked black edged around the corners of my vision, which had gone blurry.

"Tell Graves he needs to burn the pieces, too."

"I will. Stay with me. You'll be fine."

"I love you, Ami. You've been the one bright spot in my life."

"Now he gets verbose," she muttered, tying a knot in the bandages viciously tight. "Too tight. Too tight," she was saying, "but I'd rather he lose the arm than bleed out, right? I don't know how in Glorianna we're going to heal him."

"Leave me here," I managed.

She rolled her gorgeous eyes at me and seized my jaw in a surprisingly firm grip. Staring fiercely into my eyes, she spoke slowly and clearly. "No one is leaving you. Let me handle things for once. I'm not some fragile moonflower who can't survive the cold, okay?"

I smiled at that image. No, my Ami was no moonflower. She was a rose: lush, lovely, and full of lethal thorns.

The blackness swamped me and I went under.

~ 7 ~

THE PRISONERS ROARED. Rioting again. I clamped my hands over my ears, terrified that they'd find me. The guards always vanished themselves during the riots. They didn't care what the men did to each other. If we killed each other off, beat each other down, and exhausted ourselves doing it, all the better.

Just not better for the weak. The law of nature is that the weak shall be crushed by the strong.

"Come on, boy, dinnertime." Vork grinned at me through bloodied and broken teeth.

"Vork?" I asked. I'd thought he was dead. He'd died a long time ago, hadn't he?

"You'll never get strong if you don't eat." He held up my mangled arm, cheerfully taking a bite and chewing. Then offered it to me. "Want some?"

I took it, knowing he was right. I was weak and needed to be strong. I bit into my own arm, blood filling my mouth and hitting my aching stomach. It hurt and I wanted to vomit, but I took another bite, Vork grinning and nodding at me. In the distance, the prisoners roared and howled.

"Ash." Ami stood there, gowned in Glorianna pink, roses woven in her long hair. She held out her hands. "Ash, my love."

I tried to speak, but my mouth was full of blood and flesh.

Vork grabbed her, kissing her and pulling up her skirts. Ami writhed in pleasure, wanton and sensual. Moaning with abandon, she was naked, and Vork was fucking her. I tried to throw my arm aside, but I couldn't. I kept chewing, trying to swallow.

"Isn't this what you always wanted to do?" Vork asked. He sprouted claws and raked them down Ami's slim white body, parting the flesh so that black ichor poured out. She screamed in ecstasy. "Defile and corrupt."

"Drink this," Ami said. "Ash, you need to drink this."

I spit the bloody flesh out of my mouth. "Please, Ami," I begged her. "Don't."

"I'm right here. Drink this."

"No!" I flung the bloodied, ruined arm away from me. "I won't! I'd rather starve."

"You don't mean that." Ami sounded so stern. Angry with me. What had I done? I'd left her, and the undead wolves came.

"Ami!" I yelled. "Oh no, the wolves…" I couldn't yell loud enough, the words mush in my mouth.

Sharp pain cracked across my face, and I opened my eyes. Firelight. Roaring and howling resolved into a storm-tossed surf crashing outside, the wind howling through the turrets. Ami, her hair tied back, hollows in her lovely face, cradled one hand in the other. I blinked at her.

"Are you hurt?" I asked.

She made a sound, part laugh, part sob. "Who knew slapping you would mostly hurt my hand? And it wasn't nearly as fun as all those times I imagined doing it."

"I'm sorry." I tried to sit up and she easily pressed me back. So weak. But I wasn't fourteen and in the prison, easy meat for the bigger, stronger men. My arm throbbed and I lifted it so I could see. Covered in bandages. I tore at them, needing to look.

"Ash. Don't, please don't." Ami threw herself over my arm, pinning it against my body with hers. "Leave the bandages alone. Your arm was wounded—remember?"

I stared at her, not remembering anything. Why was she here in the prison? The animal need to tear off the bandages snarled inside me and I tried to push her off. She clung, stubborn as a leech.

"Leave. It. Alone." She said through gritted teeth.

I couldn't fight her. I should be able to pick her up with one hand, to be the one pinning her to the bed. With my free hand, I found her ass, naked under her nightgown. "Ami," I murmured, the animal need changing direction. "Give us a kiss."

"Oh no, you don't." She wriggled free and fetched something from the floor. A mug, which she refilled from a water jug. "You're lucid enough to drink this." She sat beside me on the bed, holding the mug to my lips.

"I don't want to drink more blood. Don't make me." I sounded so weak and whiny.

Ami's face crumpled and she smoothed back my hair. "It's just water, love. You have a fever and it's confusing you. Just water. You need to drink it."

"Don't let the men get you," I urged her. They roared outside. Howling to get in.

"They won't. We're safe. Drink some water."

Because she poured it into my mouth, I swallowed. "They do terrible things," I confided. "Don't let them know how much you hate it. They like that. It only makes them want more when you scream. When they can make you cry and plead."

"Oh, Ash," she whispered, her face gleaming with tears.

"Don't cry," I cautioned her. "Where's your knife?"

"It's here." She pointed to it on the table by the fire.

"Give it to me," I urged her.

"No way, boy-o. I'm keeping it out of your reach for now."

"They're coming. I hear them. They're right outside the door."

"That's the wind," she soothed. She poured more water into my mouth. So cool. It washed the blood and flesh away. "We're safe at Windroven."

"The twins!" I suddenly remembered. "They're under the blanket."

"They're in bed, asleep and safe. You saved them. You saved all of us, so you can sleep now."

I reached up and touched her face. She leaned into my palm, then turned to kiss it.

"So bright," I said. "My sun."

"Sleep now, Ash. Sleep and heal."

WHEN I AWOKE again, I had no idea how much time had passed, if any. The firelight burned at the same low level. The wind still howled against the shutters, making them rattle against the hinges, and the surf roared against the cliffs below. Another, deeper rumble undercut them both. Not the rioting prisoners of my nightmares, but something else.

The thrice-cursed volcano. I started to rub a hand over my face and found I couldn't move my arm. Either arm. Lifting my head from the pillow, I saw my wrists were tied with rope to the wooden sides of the bed.

And Ami slept in a chair next to me.

She'd dragged over a big armchair and curled up in it, her slight body dwarfed by the winged sides. A fur throw was draped over her lap, and her creamy nightgown sagged over one shoulder, baring skin a few shades lighter. Her rose-gold curls tumbled in wild disarray, bright against the deep velvet of the chair, her long lashes of the same color feathered against her cheeks. Slack and parted in sleep, her pink lips looked full and lush, a sexual counterpoint that belied the angelic picture she made.

Along with the soft snore that dragged out of her.

I smiled for it. She might be the image of Glorianna, but she was a flesh and blood woman, with all the foibles and flaws of one. Was that what she meant about needing me to see her?

I wished I could reach for her. But the minx had tied me down. My arm throbbed, and I surveyed the bandages. Blood had seeped through in places, but had long since dried. Probably good. Though the fever still raked at me, making me shiver despite the furs mounded on me. Weights pressing against my sides and legs must be heated stones. I moved restlessly, wanting to kick away the oppressive bulk. Ami stirred, snore halting in mid-snort, and she opened her eyes.

Wild blue, misty with sleep, her eyes found me. They cleared and sharpened. "You're awake."

"You tied me down."

"You kept trying to pull off the bandages. I had to do something." She had a funny defensive tone in her voice, and she didn't move out of the chair. Instead she curled in on herself, hands still tucked between her thighs, as if wary of me.

"I didn't hurt you, did I?"

She shook her head, mussed curls bouncing, smiling wryly. "It's funny how that's always the first thing you ask. Do you think I'm so fragile?"

Telling her that she seemed impossibly delicate to me, like

some priceless work of art that could be forever damaged if I wasn't careful, was probably the wrong thing to say, so I didn't reply to that. "Can I be untied now?"

"Oh! Yes." She flushed a little, chagrined, and uncurled with unconscious grace, fluttering her fingers over a pink-mouthed yawn. "My mind is muzzy from sleep."

"How long since the attack?" I asked as she worked to un-knot the ropes from my good arm.

She glanced up at me through a lace of bright lashes, the firelight framing her hair like a halo. "Three days. Don't get riled up or I won't untie you."

Three days? I let my head fall back, aghast at the loss of time.

"Here, drink this." She pressed a mug of water into my freed hand and slipped behind me to help prop me up.

"What about my other arm?"

"Drink your water and this tea first. If you're good, I'll think about it." She sounded prim, but she pressed a fleeting kiss to my temple. Chaste enough, but the contact—and her round breast pressed into my side—had my blood heating for her, as always. Such was her magic over even my fever-battered flesh.

I drank the water and traded the mug for one with lukewarm tea. It tasted bitter and I recognized the herb as one for reducing fever. At least I wasn't delirious anymore. I vaguely remembered nightmares. Hopefully I hadn't said too much in my ranting.

"How bad?" I asked her.

"The attack? We lost three men. The Tala nurses didn't even come to Windroven—they took off for Annfwn, calling *this* a land of monsters." She smiled when I coughed out a laugh. "I found that deliciously ironic, too, and have been waiting all this time to share it with you."

"Injured?"

"Skunk took some bites, but is on his feet. You're the worst." Her gaze went to my bandaged arm, and I drained the mug, handing it back to her.

"I need to see it," I told her, determined to undo the knots myself if she balked. I felt much stronger. She wouldn't be able to wrestle me down again. I cocked a brow at her. "Did you really pin me down?"

She slipped off the bed, running fingers through her hair, trying to tame it. Looking around, she found a ribbon and tied it back again. "I had to," she said. "You kept thrashing around, trying to get up."

I got the knots undone and lifted my arm. Heavy, stiff and unresponsive. Had I been smart, I'd have thrust the other arm in the beast's mouth. Stupid to use my sword arm.

"You should have gotten Graves or one of the other men to sit with me," I told her, as I unwound the bandages. The padding stuck to the dried blood and pus. Infection from that toxic shit those creatures had for blood. Wonderful.

Ami brought over a basin of warm water and set it beside me, then soaked a cloth in it. "Might as well clean it up and change the bandages, since you're determined to mess with it," she explained.

It was bad. I made myself study the shredded flesh as I would with one of my patients. It helped that the damaged limb looked nothing like my own arm. It looked, in fact, uncannily like the one in the nightmares, and my stomach lurched at the now vivid memory, the tea roiling.

Ami thrust an empty basin at me just in time, holding it as I puked up the water and tea I'd drunk—and not much else but bitter bile. I lay back, drenched in cold sweat, taking the mug she handed me, watching her take the basin away and empty it. No fit duty for a queen.

"I'm sorry," I managed. She sat beside me again, laying a cool cloth on my brow that felt like heaven.

"The acquired skills of motherhood," she said. "I can see a puking coming from a league away. And stop apologizing. You took care of me when I was hurt."

"I wasn't kind to you, though." I'd been cruel to her. Snarky and deliberately crude, so busy fighting my lust and longing that I hadn't even tried to be gentle.

"True," she replied, brows arched. "You were awful—and exactly what I needed, spoiled, bratty princess that I was." She laid the cloth over my eyes. "Now lie still while I wrap this up again."

"No." I dragged the cloth off, struggling to sit up.

"Ash…"

"I need to look at it."

"Oh, because that was such a great idea," she snapped.

"Keep the puke basin handy." I tried for a smile, the scar tissue on my face pulling. The fever had me stiff and sore all over, even the old wounds I'd thought long since forgotten.

"You can't heal yourself, so what good does it do? You're only tormenting yourself."

I didn't reply, forcing myself to study the rent muscle and torn ligaments, stitched together with black thread. I had to know how bad it was. Also, though I couldn't heal myself the way I could others, the shapeshifter blood from my father did allow me to heal faster. Pus oozed out between the stitches, fresh blood, too, here and there, where removing the caked bandages had broken the scabs. The main forearm bone seemed solid, though the minor one had likely snapped in a few places.

"Who did the stitches?" I asked.

Ami lifted her chin, the set of it defiant. "I did."

I'd figured. "Is Windroven empty of staff?"

She dipped her chin reluctantly. "Not entirely empty, but nearly so. You were right. I was a prideful fool in insisting on coming here."

"You had your reasons, Ami. Don't upset yourself."

Her mouth dropped open. "How can you say that? I nearly got us all killed! You almost died, Ash, and it would have been all my fault."

"No, it would have been the fault of those *Deyrr* creatures. Now hand me that knife."

~ 8 ~

"WHEN DANU GROWS pink roses!" she exclaimed, using the High Queen's favorite curse, and making me laugh. "Don't you laugh—you've been trying to get your hands on that knife for three days. I was sure you were going to try to kill yourself with it." Her eyes welled with unshed tears and she looked away, swallowing hard.

"I need to release the stitches, to let the infection out," I told her gently.

"Oh." She sounded small and sad. Then got up and fetched the knife. "Maybe I should do it."

I eyed her, but she looked steady enough. "All right. But do a tourniquet on my upper arm first, if you would."

"The easy part," she sighed, then followed my instructions, tying and tightening a piece of rope above my elbow.

She laid a cloth over her lap and eased my mangled arm onto it, then dragged the lantern closer. Picking at the stitches, she cut them, then dragged them painfully free. I lay back, glad she'd offered as I might not have gotten through it on my own.

"I tried to get it clean," she said. "I did my best."

"You did well," I told her, staring at the ceiling and taming my churning gut. "The ichor in those creatures is toxic. I saw it back in Ordnung after we defeated Illyria. Even a trained healer—one without magic—couldn't have done better. We just need to drain, clean and disinfect it. Did you set the bone?"

"I wasn't sure how and I was afraid I'd do more damage by trying. Mostly I wanted you to stop bleeding."

"I'm sorry, Ami."

"Would you stop apologizing?" She rubbed away some tears with her forearm, and continued working. "I wanted to do it. It was the least I could do."

"You don't owe me anything." I hissed as she pulled hard on one of the stitches.

"Serves you right, you ass," she muttered. "There. Shall I help you wash it or are you determined to do that all yourself, too?"

"You could hand me the puke basin."

She did, brow creasing when I laid my arm over it and moved the lot to put in my lap. The blood and pus—along with some thrice-cursed black ichor—flowed more freely, but not enough. We had no evidence the ichor could make undead without *Deyrr* rituals to power the transformation, but it did create infection and I needed it out of me. "Knife, please."

"What are you doing?"

I set my teeth, wishing I had a stick to clench in them, but it might upset Ami too much if I asked for that. "I need to cut it open more."

"Oh, Ash." She looked a little green.

"Don't look."

"I don't think I can." She stayed where she was, steadfastly staring at the fire.

Fortunately—though I might not think so in the future—my arm was mangled enough that more pain didn't make an appreciable difference. I cut some slices, letting the blood, pus, and ichor drain out, feeling lightheaded, but thankfully I remained sharp enough to avoid cutting open any major blood vessels.

"I finally understand how you could have cut the brand off your face and set it on fire," Ami remarked, sneaking occasional glances. "Though I don't know where that kind of will comes from."

"From the fires of hell," I commented without thinking. It hurt considerably. At least some nerves were still alive, right? Then I caught Ami's stricken expression and wished I could unsay it. "That was a joke."

She regarded me steadily, gaze fixed on mine. "I know it wasn't."

I had said things then. I couldn't face the pity in her eyes, focusing instead on the chewed mess of my arm. It said something, that facing it was easier. "I need to pour water over this."

"I can do that." She came around to get the wash basin. "Ash—you're really pale."

Sheathed in cold, stinking sweat, too. "Gotta get this done or I'll lose the arm." Or die. Still a distinct possibility, but I didn't want Ami to worry.

"Lie back and let me wash it."

I might have to let her do it. I was getting dizzy. I lay back on the mounded pillows. "Then pour alcohol on it," I told her.

"What?"

"Do we have any—besides the Feast of Moranu wine the duchess sent?"

"Yes, but won't that hurt?"

Oh yeah, speaking of the fires of hell. "A stick to clench in my teeth would be helpful," I admitted. Better that than for her to hear me screaming. "Better yet, get Graves to do this. You go get some sleep."

"I'm doing this." She sounded terse, her face averted, but also dug in. I wouldn't change her mind.

"The clearer and less flavored the alcohol, the better," I said.

She nodded, pulled on a robe, and taking the lantern with her, went out the door.

I lay there, looking around the room. Her room, the one she'd shared with Hugh during their short marriage, and the one she'd given birth to the twins in, but not the same bed. That one had been a fancy of gold leaf, trailing ribbons, lace curtains, and pink roses. This one was plainer, though still high quality, carved from dark wood to look like the polished limbs of a tree. It made me wonder when she'd changed it.

Sitting up a little, I drank more water and the fever tea, hoping they'd stay down this time. Then, while she was gone, I felt around for the pieces of the minor arm bone. Splintered all right, and I couldn't set them. By the feel of it, there wasn't enough of it left. I should be grateful the major bone was intact. If I lived through this I'd have to train myself to wield a sword with the other arm. This one would never have the same ability to grip again.

The door opened and Ami entered, a basket over her arm. "I brought broth and bread, too, in case you can keep it down," she said.

I'd need the strength. "If you don't mind, I'll eat that first." I should be honest with her. "It's possible I'll pass out when you hit it with the alcohol. Don't stop. Douse all of it."

Pale, she firmed her lips and nodded. She poured soup from a tall container into a bowl and handed it to me. I cupped it in my hand and drank, the warm broth salty and intense with marrow, my bones feeling as if they drank it up.

"Should I stitch it up again?" she asked.

I shook my head and held out the bowl for more. Pursing her lips dubiously, she refilled it. "Not unless anything is really gushing blood. Just, if you can stomach it, try to line up the loose flesh again so the edges match. Then loosely wrap up the whole thing and let it seep."

"I wish I was better at this." She studied me. "It feels so wrong that you've healed so many people—saved their lives—and there's no one to help you. I tried to send for someone, but…"

"Snowed in?" I cocked my head at the howling wind. "You got your Mornai storm."

"Don't laugh about this." She clenched her fists. "I know how stupid I am that I caused this. I don't expect you to forgive me."

"Ami," I tossed aside the empty bowl and caught the sleeve of her robe before she could flee. She looked surprised that I moved so fast. "There's nothing to forgive."

She firmed her pretty mouth. "Maybe not for you, but I have a great deal to reconcile with myself. Anything else before we do this?"

"A couple of shots of the alcohol might be good."

"On a virtually empty stomach and you with a fever still?" She frowned at me.

"Hard to screw myself up any more at this point," I pointed out. "And it'll dull the edge, at least a little."

She poured some of the liquor into the empty mug and I tossed it back, hissing at the harsh burn. "Branlian whiskey?"

"The closest thing we had to what you asked for." Ami shrugged. Then poured herself a draught and drank it. "For courage," she said with a grimace.

"You don't have to do this," I told her.

"Yes, I do." She handed me a wooden spoon for stirring stews and I took it. Paused before setting it between my teeth.

"No matter what, don't stop," I said.

"I know."

"I mean, even if I'm screaming."

"Oh." She considered. "Even weakened you're so much stronger than I am—should we tie you down again?"

Much as I hated the thought, I grimly agreed. She retrieved the rope and secured the upper part of my wounded arm to the bed post, then tied my good hand to the headboard. I wrapped my fist around the binding rope, hanging on. That would help, too. She picked up the spoon and I opened my mouth to bite on it, but she hesitated, eyes a stormy blue.

"Last chance to back out." I said it as gently as I could.

She gave me a long look, then smiled. Not all that nicely. "If you scream, I'll just consider it payback for all the times you've pissed me off."

That's my girl. I clamped my back teeth on the spoon and lay back.

~ *9* ~

I MUST HAVE lost consciousness early on, because I awoke to daylight, not remembering much beyond a haze of burning agony. The spoon was gone, I was untied, and my injured arm lay across my belly, lightly swathed in bandages. It ached, but with a fierce bright pain I actually welcomed. It was the crawling, stretching kind of pain that meant healing had begun.

Thank Glorianna. And Her avatar.

I was hungry, too—another good sign—and the fever had lessened. It still buzzed at the edges, making me feel a little chilled, but my vision had lost that too-acute sharpness. The wind howled outside, but from a direction that didn't rattle the shutters as much. The white light filtered through the cracks in them, and showed through the glass-sealed clerestory windows that ringed the room near the ceiling. Nothing to see but snowflakes dashing themselves against the glass, like beasts starving to get in, but I frowned at them. I didn't remember the windows.

The door creaked open, and Ami peeked in. "You're awake? Are you up for small, tremendously annoying visitors?"

Stella had already stuck her head around Ami, wedging her small body through the space. "Ash!" she shouted, popping through like a cork and racing toward me.

"Slowly and gently!" Ami commanded, her voice as steely as any general's. Stella froze, then stepped toward the bed with exaggeratedly slow, prancing steps. Ami had caught Astar by the back of his sweater, swooping him up and carrying him over. She'd bathed and changed clothes, her hair in loosely spilling curls and her eyes bright. "Be careful, both of you. Anyone who jostles Ash and makes him hurt loses all their Feast of Moranu presents."

The kids exchanged wide-eyed looks and nodded. Ami set Astar next to me on the bed, then lifted Stella up. She stuck her small fingers in her mouth and stared at me. I tried to keep my emotions calm, in case she could sense them.

"Does it hurt?" Astar asked, pointing at my arm.

"A little bit," I answered, not sure how honest to be.

"You killed the wolf before it could eat us," Astar informed me.

I glanced at Ami who made a face. No telling them what they saw wasn't real. It might have been nice to keep them innocent of the more vile aspects of the world a little longer though. "I did," I agreed, "and now it can never hurt either one of you again."

"I don't ever want to be a wolf," Stella popped her fingers out of her mouth to say. "And you hurt a whole lot. It stinks." Fat tears began to roll down her face.

Not an easy magic to have, Stella's gift of empathy. "It's not a real smell—that's the magic's way of showing you emotion. And it feels stronger to you than to him," Ami consoled the girl, stroking her dark curls. "Ash is very strong and tough. He can withstand more pain than anyone I've ever known. Look at him—he's smiling."

Stella eyed me tearfully, stuck her fingers back in her mouth and jumped off the bed, turning into a mountain lion cub on the way, and tearing out the door as if her tail were on fire. Ami sighed and watched her go. "I was afraid that would happen, but she insisted on seeing you. She could feel your pain, so there was no lying to her about it. And what Nilly wants, Willy must have, too."

"I want to learn to use a sword," Astar announced, blissfully unbothered, "so I can kill wolves." He jumped up to demonstrate with an invisible sword, thrusting it wildly in the air and bouncing the bed.

"*No jostling.*" The lash of Ami's reprimand caught him mid-bounce and he tucked his hands behind his back, pasting on an angelic smile the mirror of his mother's.

Then he turned back to me. "Will you teach me to use a sword, Ash—will you?"

Ouch. I glanced at Ami, who wouldn't meet my eye. "Maybe someday," I told him.

"Does that mean tomorrow?" he asked hopefully.

"That means someday," Ami corrected crisply, "and that's enough visiting." She scooped him up, but he struggled, reaching for me.

"I want to stay!"

"Ash needs to rest. Go find Nilly and make sure she's not being naughty."

He brightened at that and tore out the door, shouting, "Nilly Nilly Nilly!"

Ami shook her head and sighed, giving me a rueful smile. "Sorry about that and thank you—they were driving me crazy, worrying about you."

"That's all right. It was good to see them."

"Yes. Well." She studied me. "How do you feel, really? I

know it must be bad if you reduced Nilly to tears inside of a minute, so don't bother lying."

"I really do feel better. The arm is improved and the fever not so high. It hurts, sure, but it's healing."

She pursed her lips, then poured some of the fever tea and handed me the mug. "Well, your color *is* better. And your eyes are back to your normal bright green, not glowing like a cat's in the dark."

I paused mid-sip. "They were glowing?"

"Shapeshifter magic or something, but I could see the light on my skin, even."

I contemplated that, not sure what it meant. So much I still didn't know about my heritage. "I'll have to ask some of the Tala healers about that."

"When you go back to Annfwn," she said, matter-of-fact, no question in it, busying herself with laying out some soup. I didn't bother to correct her that I hadn't decided where I'd go. She brought the soup over on a tray, setting it on my lap and taking the empty mug. "After you eat, we'll look at the arm."

"You don't have to wait on me, Ami. You're a queen, not a servant." I knew I sounded irritable, but I hadn't quite expected her to be so ready to have me gone. Silly, as I'd been meant to be long gone before this.

She flashed me an opaque look that didn't fool me. I'd annoyed her with that. "We're snowed in at a virtually empty castle—believe me, the calls to hear petitions and attend social engagements have gone way down."

"That's not what I meant." I rubbed my forehead, where the fever made it throb, regretting that I'd spoken.

"I know what you meant, but you'll have to put up with my company for a while longer. Though now that you're reasonably lucid, if cranky with it, I might get some of the maids or men at arms to spell me."

Lucid. I frowned at her, remembering those nightmares.

"Now that you aren't saying things you wouldn't want anyone else to hear," she clarified, pointedly, still expectant.

I wasn't sure how to ask, certain I didn't want to hear the answer. But I knew Ami and she had that look about her, like she had her teeth into something and wouldn't be dropping it. "Did I—" My throat caught and I coughed, swallowed some broth to ease it. "During the fever, was I…"

She raised her finely arched brows, waiting for me to finish. When I couldn't think of any words, I stared at my soup. It held no answers either.

Ami sat on the bed and covered my good hand with hers. "Ash," she said, and the hesitation in her voice, the sympathy, had me wanting to crawl away. "What happened to you in that prison?"

"I've told you about that," I said.

"Not really." She tightened her hand on mine. I knew she wanted me to turn mine over, to lace our fingers together and return the grip, but I couldn't make myself. More than anything I wanted her to go away, to leave me alone and not ask these questions. Not something I could ask for without driving her away forever and I wasn't ready to face that. Still too sick and weak. I'd walked away from her before and it had taken all I had. I couldn't do it again, not yet.

"Ash," Ami said with more asperity. "Don't do this. Don't retreat inside that silence. You can talk to me."

"There's nothing to talk about. You know everything already."

"You told me about the staged matches. How the old Tala

man taught you to fight, how to channel the beast inside to grow strong and fast. You said the guards would whip you when you disobeyed."

I laughed a little, the grate of it painful in my chest. "Or just when they felt like it. Disobedience is in the eye of the beholder."

"But there's more, isn't there? You said you were in there ten years and you were twenty-three when you got out, which means you were little more than a boy in there."

"A lot of us were young. Uorsin's law didn't discriminate based on age."

"I'm naïve about a lot of things, Ash, but not about everything. Some of the things you said—"

They do terrible things. It only makes them want more when you scream. When they can make you cry and plead.

"Don't speak them," I grated out. Glancing up at her lovely face, I saw what I'd dreaded most. That pity.

"Ash, I'm so sorry," she said, her voice full of compassion.

"Don't be," I said, harshly enough that she physically flinched. I pulled my hand from hers on pretext of eating more soup, but it shook too much to hold the spoon, so I picked up the bowl and drank. Not smart because I dumped half of it down the front of my nightshirt. Growling in frustrated rage, I hurled the bowl at the wall, where it shattered with a crash, the ceramic pieces raining to the floor.

Ami didn't look, just stared at me, lips pressed together tightly enough to make them go white as snow, eyes shadowed blue pools. Then she stood and shook out her skirts. "I'll just get a broom and—"

"Leave it." It came out as a barked command, making her jump.

"Fine," she bit out. In a flurry of rustling skirts and bouncing curls, she left, the faint scent of roses lingering behind.

I hated that, hated that I'd frightened her. But this was better, wasn't it? She should be afraid of me. She needed to see what kind of foul and twisted creature she'd taken to her bed. Then it would be easier for us both to say goodbye.

As soon as I got my strength back, I'd go.

~ 10 ~

I SLEPT ON and off all day. Ami sent Skunk to help me, the young guardsman irritatingly cheerful about his own injuries. Still, he had the strength to brace me to use the chamber pot—a good thing as I was weaker than I'd thought. Standing up nearly had me on the floor. Would have, if he hadn't caught me.

Preparations for the Feast of Moranu—already the following night—sounded to be well underway. And Windroven wasn't as badly staffed as I'd feared, or as Ami had made it sound. Could be that had been a product of my fever-muddled brain.

That first venture out of bed exhausted me enough that I crashed into sleep as soon as Skunk got me back in it. When I woke again, I remembered that I'd driven Ami off before she could unwrap my arm to check it. The light had dimmed considerably, likely late afternoon sliding into evening, the blizzard raging unabated. The sound had leaked into my dreams with its roaring and howling.

It only makes them want more when you scream. When they can make you cry and plead.

The worst possible time for those ugly old memories to rear their monstrous heads. I'd put all that behind me. Maimed and scarred myself to do it. Taken refuge with the monks and a vow of silence to quiet that howling within. Wretchedly unfair that they should return to haunt me now.

Perhaps Glorianna had determined to punish me for my infidelity to Her. When I'd broken my vow, it had been—at least in part, I'd justified to myself—to help Her avatar. And the goddess had seemed to be in favor of that. But I'd strayed from Her exclusive service too long. Overstayed my welcome with Ami and tested Glorianna's patience.

The goddess had reminded me that I remained a savage, twisted beast in my heart, and there would be no healing from that.

It was awkward to do alone, but I got the bandages off, studying the arm in the low light. A bruised and bloodied mangled mess. More purple and black now, and distorted with swelling. But I could at least wiggle my fingers, if not fully flex them. The movement pulled with agonizing tightness. No fresh blood welled, however—and no sign of pus or the black ichor. The flesh seemed to be knitting together well enough.

The chamber door creaked, opening a hand's width, and a mountain lion cub strolled in on too-big paws, surveying me with predatory eyes the same color as her mother's. "Heya, little Nilly," I said, surprised to see her back already. I'd figured she'd avoid me for days yet. "Have you been a cub all this time? You know that's not good for you." I wondered if Ami knew.

She padded over and leapt onto the bed, craning her neck to sniff at my arm, and I braced myself. Her muzzle wrinkled in feline disgust. But she climbed up onto my lap, nudging my good hand with her head, so I rubbed her ears. A purr welled up and she draped herself over my lap, nudging at the wounded arm, which I'd moved aside. She reached out a cupped paw, tapping my arm, trying to pull it closer.

"Silly Nilly," I whispered. "What are you doing?"

She purred louder and determinedly wrapped both paws around my forearm, rolling onto her back and dragging it to lay across her furry fawn-colored belly. I winced in anticipation of her going into a feline attack of hind claws and biting, but she licked my arm, rubbing her whiskers against it.

And the pain eased. So much so that the sudden abatement startled me. Drowsiness followed, irresistible and dragging. Unable to resist, I fell into a deep sleep.

"HERE YOU ARE. Bad kitty!" Ami was whispering, trying to be quiet. She had been—it was Nilly's growl that brought me to instant alert. "I mean it, Stella," Ami hissed. "You come here right now, young lady. You know you weren't supposed to come in here."

"It's all right," I said, and Ami glanced up, startled. She had hold of two of Stella's paws, trying to ease her out from under my arm. "Though she's probably been a cub long enough. I've lost track of time." I squinted at the clerestory windows, which had gone dark, white flakes hurling themselves against the glass and into the shadows again.

"We've been searching the entire castle for *hours*." Ami planted fists on hips, glaring at her daughter in exasperation. "Someone isn't getting any dessert if she's still a cub, I know that."

Stella popped into human shape again—wriggling and naked toddler—throwing her arms around my neck and planting a kiss on my cheek. "Ash," she proclaimed.

"Yes, sweetheart," I gave her a one-armed hug. "Go with your mother now."

She planted one more kiss on me, jumped off the bed, neatly ducking Ami's grab with shapeshifter speed, and darted out the door, black hair flying and tiny butt twitching. Ami stared after her in dismay. "I'll be so happy when she learns the Tala trick of shifting back with something to wear. She's a princess, not a naked hoyden."

"She's a baby," I replied. "She can run around naked for a few more years before she has to worry about her gowns all the time."

The wrong thing to say because Ami fixed me with a withering glare. Oh—that's right—she was no doubt still mad at me from before. "She is *not* a baby," Ami informed me. "Not anymore. And you spoiling her won't help her character any. I should know."

"You're not spoiled, Ami."

"I was—something you pointed out any number of times."

"Well, I was wrong. How many times do you want me to apologize for how badly I treated you?" I needed to get up and move. I threw back the covers, and swung my legs over.

"What do you think you're doing?"

"If we're going to fight, I want to do it standing up. I'm tired of lying abed." *Like a weakling.* I didn't say it but Ami's expression softened. "Plus I have to piss, so you might want to absent yourself."

"Do you need help?"

"No, I don't need help." Though once behind the screen, I leaned against the wall. She didn't say anything, which made me think she'd left. But when I emerged, she was sitting in the armchair she'd slept in while keeping vigil, looking forlorn and far too young.

"I don't even understand why we're fighting all the time,"

she said, sadly enough to wrench my heart.

I blew out a breath, sat heavily on the side of the bed. "Because I'm an ass."

She smiled a little, as I'd hoped, but grew solemn again. "You *are* an ass, but that's not it. We just can't seem to stop taking bites out of each other and I don't understand why."

"Maybe because we'd resolved to part ways and now we're forced together again because of this." I lifted my arm as I said it. "We know in our hearts that we shouldn't be together, and so—"

Ami's eyes had grown wide. "Ash!" she interrupted. "Your *arm*."

I looked at it, ready to see whatever new damage had appeared, but it... looked so much better. No longer so bruised, the lacerations more knitted together. Experimentally, I flexed and curled my fingers, finding I could very nearly make a fist. I met Ami's astonished gaze.

"Stella," I said. "Guess she has healing abilities along with the empathy."

Ami stared back, then dropped her gaze to my arm. "What does that mean for her?" Then she jumped up. "If she's anything like you after a healing session, she's going to be dead on her feet."

She flew out the door and I followed—more slowly, but far faster than I'd have guessed I'd be capable of. I didn't have to chase her far. Ami stood in the hall, then glanced back over her shoulder with a smile. The torchlight danced through her tumbling curls and her eyes danced with amusement and love.

My heart turned over, and I had to catch my breath at the emotion she stirred in me.

Holding my injured arm tight against my chest, I eased up

behind her to find Stella, still naked, curled up in a ball in the middle of the hallway, little fingers tucked firmly in her mouth, fast asleep.

"We'll have to watch her," I murmured with a sigh. "She'll want to heal anyone she perceives as hurting. It won't be good for her growth if she drains herself too much or too often."

Ami crouched and gathered her daughter up, pressing a kiss to the girl's brow. "Not just anyone," she said, then fastened her gaze on me. "She loves you. We all do, you know."

Why that sounded like an accusation, I didn't know.

"Since you're up and so spry," she continued, "you can join me for supper. Half an hour in the main hall."

"I—"

"Your queen commands you," Ami cut me off in an arch tone. "And take a bath. Nilly is right about that. You stink."

~ 11 ~

T HOUGH I MINDED the high-handedness of Ami's command, it did feel good to bathe. Skunk hauled in water for
me and I used the queen's own brass tub to scrub more than
four days of fever stink and old blood off of me. Ami's bed was
a mess, now that I had my head again enough to notice, so I
wryly suggested that Skunk might get some of the maids up to
change the sheets and freshen the chambers while I was out.

I'd fouled her bed long enough. Which very well might have
been Ami's intent in prying me out of her chambers to go down
and eat in the first place.

Skunk helped me dress in some loose fitting pants and shirt
in Avonlidgh purple, which made me think they'd been Hugh's.
But my own clothing consisted mainly of fighting leathers and a
couple more formal uniforms Ami had arranged for me, so I
wouldn't shame her. Those were in a nondescript soft black.
Dressing me in Avonlidgh colors would be as problematic as me
wearing Tala bloodred. And of course, I still had the white robes
of my order, folded at the very bottom of my trunk.

So many allegiances, none of them exactly my own. But that
had ever been my life. Part-blood, never more than half in any
world, never fully belonging to anything. Except in prison,
ironically enough. There I fit right in, along with every other

114

mostly savage man incarcerated with me.

I didn't object to the clothes, though I was taller than Hugh had been, so the cuffs came up a bit short on me. Stuffed into my worn indoor boots of folded Tala leather, the pants didn't look so bad, and with my arm in the sling Skunk helped me fashion, I ended up rolling the shirtsleeves up anyway.

The good thing about having a man like Skunk assist—he didn't blink when I asked for my short blade. He helped me cinch the belt over my shirt so I could reach the blade easily with my good hand. Finally I didn't feel naked.

I'd rather have my sword, but I wouldn't be able to draw it in my current state. For the first time since I got a good look at the injury, though, I felt optimistic that I might be able to use that arm again—with Stella's healing help. Hopefully what she'd instinctively done already would make all the difference. I wouldn't call on her again. She was far too young to drain herself so. Over time, she'd learn to pace herself, and to build in time for the deep sleep needed for recovery from healing another. Right now, though, she needed her energy to grow into an adult, not to help others.

Spoiling her won't help her character any. I should know.

Had Ami been like Stella at that age? I didn't think so. Ami had been motherless, raised by her much older sisters, and—with her celebrated beauty apparent even at birth, so the stories went—a petted darling of the court. She didn't have Stella's inherent Tala wildness or the compassion of being an empath. But behind that bright and laughing façade, Ami was sensitive in ways most people didn't perceive.

I contemplated that as I walked down to the main hall, wending my way through Windroven's twisting stone corridors and down steps with gentle divots at the center, engraved by generations of footsteps. People had lived here at least four centuries, so perhaps Ami was right, the ever-present rumbling of the volcano might mean nothing.

But then again, those had been centuries when magic had been confined behind the barrier around Annfwn. Not eddying and surging as it was these days, waking all sorts of monsters. Like those wolf creatures, wherever they'd been conjured or created from. And very likely, given what had happened at Nahanau, a dragon sleeping in the depths below us.

What staff remained in the castle had been busy, apparently, for the graceful old hallways were draped with new-looking silk moonflower garlands, dangling with crystals carved to look like snowflakes. No doubt those were the duchess's contribution. White candles burned in antique sconces tarnished black with age and set in niches that seemed to have been designed for exactly that purpose. Those might be as old as the walls they decorated. There was a comfort in that, the continuity of it. Something, I reflected, that had never been a part of my life.

Perhaps that's what Ami had connected to at Windroven. In many ways, she had little more history than I did. Daughter of an upstart conqueror who built his castle on the bones of another, and daughter, too, of a queen who had abandoned her people to live in a foreign land.

Endings and new beginnings were part of the celebration of the Feast of Moranu. In my youth, we all helped clean our small cottage from top to bottom. The scent of soap and vinegar unexpectedly came back to me, a background for the spiced bread my mother baked and the hot wax of candles my parents lit at sundown. Then we wrote or drew images of what we wanted to leave behind with the old year, things we felt bad about or wrongs done us that we needed to let go of.

Funny to remember that now, as I'd never practiced the custom in all the years since. In prison, time went by unmarked by celebrations of any kind, grinding along like a stone wheel over grain, reducing us to spineless ash. The White Brothers, of course, looked to Glorianna, so while they marked her sister Moranu's feast, they did not observe with more than a lit candle.

My parents, though, kept the candles and fire blazing high, holding vigil in silence and reflection until midnight. Not a thing a kid stays awake for very well, and I'd only made it once, that last winter before Father died. But they always wakened me a bit before midnight, and we'd take what we'd written and a candle each, then go out to the village square where the bonfire towered with hot flame. Keeping silent, our neighbors would throw their remembrances into the fire—sometimes fancy scrolls, other times bits of leather or bark. Occasionally someone tossed in an object.

Then we'd wait, holding the candles up to the sky in our cupped palms—toward Moranu's moon if it was in the sky that year. We were supposed to concentrate on our hopes for the coming year. Mostly I'd be curious about what everyone else threw into the fire, imagining stories behind the occasional object I glimpsed. Back then my hopes had been confined to thinking about the iced spiced bread that awaited me. Odd to remember, too, that time when I'd been innocent enough for hope not to be a jagged blade that tore me from the inside out.

At the stroke of midnight, the village elders doused the bonfire, and we blew out our candles. We'd stand there in the abrupt darkness, shivering with winter chill, smoke billowing and burning my nose. Then, one by one, people relit their candles, passing the flame from one to the next, until the darkness was illuminated again by all the candles reflecting on faces now wreathed in smiles.

Many of the adults stayed up until dawn, keeping the candles alight and celebrating with drinking and dancing. I'd never seen that part. I would have been just getting old enough when everything changed. Shaking myself from the reverie, I hurried on, certain I must be late, and they'd be waiting supper on me.

I paused at one of the rare glassed-in windows, the big one that looked east, on a high floor with a grand foyer before it. Several staircases led onto the foyer, making a landing of the otherwise unused space. I'd always figured it for a lookout point, but it had been decorated for the feast, tall candelabras and torchieres ringing the space, garlands hanging from the walls. Snow piled deep on the sills, the night beyond nearly white with the swirling flakes illuminated by the glow from the castle.

Entering the main hall, I found only Ami present. She stood near the great fire, and turned at the sound of my bootsteps, a mug of wine cupped in her hands. She looked radiantly lovely— more so than usual—in a gown of deep purple, scattered with stars. Jewels fashioned to look the same as those decorating her skirts draped over her wrists and delicate collarbones, which always made me think of a white-winged bird about to take flight.

I halted, clearing my throat. "I didn't realize I should have dressed up."

She smiled ruefully and waved a hand, dismissing the elaborate gown. "No, I was silly to do it. This is—" She shook her head at something and drummed up a different smile, a brighter one to cover whatever emotion had choked her up. "It's the Eve of Moranu's Feast, you know. Or maybe you don't, being sick and asleep so much."

"I didn't realize. Though I wondered when I saw all the

candles." This room, too, had candles glowing their simple flames from the niches, all the way up to the ceiling, which gave the feeling of stars shining from the shadows. "When I was a kid, we only ever lit them the night of the feast," I offered, feeling awkward.

Interest lit her face. "Oh? At Ordnung they stayed lit for a week. For all the parties and everything. It was always such a mad whirl…" She trailed off, clearly realizing my life would have been nothing like that. I tried to think of something to reassure her. I wondered if I should go change clothes.

"Anyway," she said into the suddenly uncomfortable silence. "I've had this dress for nearly two years, made for this occasion, and I've never gotten to wear it. So…" She shrugged, her fair shoulders gleaming like moonlight against the deep hue of the velvet, her breasts rising in tantalizing curves above the indecently low neckline. "I thought, might as well. At the rate I was going, it would have hung in my closet here forever, unworn. And it's so pretty." She stroked a hand over the full skirt, a sensuous caress that went through me like fire, reminding me of how she'd once touched me. "It would have been just sad to only leave it for the moths to eat."

She lifted the mug in a toast. "Happy Eve of Moranu, Ash. May the goddess bless you."

Feeling like an ass—more than usual—I picked up the other empty mug and filled it, toasting her in return. "Happy Eve to you as well, Amelia. I have no doubt Moranu is terribly jealous that Glorianna claimed you all to Herself."

Ami blinked back some dampness, her eyes a luminous blue. "You say the loveliest things when you put your mind to it."

Which wasn't nearly often enough, I knew. I searched for something else to say to please her, but most of what came to mind fell into treacherous territory. "Where are Willy and Nilly?" I asked instead.

"Asleep." Ami raised her elegant brows in significant delight. "Nilly hasn't awakened, and if she's like you after healing, I'm sure she'll sleep straight through till morning. And Astar went down an hour ago, the consequence of diligent practice over hours with a garden stake he found and declared to be his sword."

I groaned at that. "I'm sorry. I wish they hadn't seen that."

She cocked her head, a curling tendril falling against her temple. She'd put her hair up somehow, with more of the stars in it. I wondered where she'd dressed, as I'd been in her rooms.

"I'm not sorry," Ami was saying, and I dragged my thoughts back to the topic. "The twins were born into dangerous times and I doubt that will change any time soon. It's good for them to see that there are men like you—men of integrity, honor, and courage—who will risk everything to protect them from the monsters."

I studied my wine, bemused by her description of me. Not how I saw myself.

"Astar might as well start learning to hold his 'sword' correctly, as he's so determined," Ami added, pouring us both more wine. "Maybe you can get him started." *Before you go*, she didn't say, but we both heard the words anyway, our gazes catching on each other with a heated intensity that went to my core.

Once, I would have given into that heat between us, likely dashing our wine cups aside and bearing her back onto the table, pushing up her fancy gown and burying myself in her sweet cunt until she screamed with pleasure and—I shook my head hard to dispel the image. I drained my wine and set it down to find Ami still staring at me, color high on her cheeks and eyes deeper blue with desire.

"I'll carve him a wooden sword," I heard myself saying. "Tomorrow. It can be his feast gift. I don't have anything for either of them yet." Gifts. Likely people who weren't peasants gave beautiful presents, not the hand-written promises my parents and I had exchanged.

"Can you carve one handed?" Ami asked, sounding breathless.

Was this what normal parents did, sublimated their unwise lust in discussions of gifts for the children? Not that we were normal parents—or that I was a parent at all—nor did I have any clue what parents who weren't mine did.

"Skunk will help me," I replied. "And I'll think of something for Nilly."

She nodded. "I have several things for each of them."

"Good." The strange conversation, so full of things we were saying under the words, lapsed.

"Are you ready to eat?" Ami finally asked, gesturing to the table. Two places were set at the end of the long table, not as elaborate as at Lianore, but with more candles set in long holders of tarnished metal that looked like old wood, twisting and dense. Fresh-blooming flowers sat in little water-filled vases, making me wonder where Ami had gotten them. Domes of cut crystal covered the plates.

"I told the staff we'd serve ourselves." Ami glanced away, blushing. Had she also thought something like my momentary fantasy would occur? It certainly had enough times that she'd have learned to predict me. Except that we'd agreed to part ways, so she shouldn't have expected anything of the kind. Right?

"Of course," I said, and pulled out the chair at the head of the table for her.

"No, you sit there. I'll take this one." She moved to the chair immediately to the right.

"The queen should sit at the head of the table in her own castle."

"It's just us. I hardly see that it matters."

"At a formally set dinner at the big table in the main hall?" She knew how to do this Eve of the Feast of Moranu properly and I didn't. "It obviously matters."

"I just wanted things to be pretty and it's not as if there are dining tables for two in this place. Not elegant ones. It was this, the kitchens, or our rooms."

That's what we'd done in those few short days before we went after Stella—eaten in her rooms, feeding each other, usually in bed. The memories both warmed me and filled me with regret. Everywhere else we'd been, we'd eaten with other people.

"Where did you and Hugh eat?" I asked, before I thought to stop myself.

Ami gave me a funny look, still standing beside the chair she'd picked. "Here. If it was just the two of us, he'd sit there and I'd sit here."

So formal their marriage had been. It made me angry for her sake, and unreasonably jealous for my own. Sitting in Hugh's clothes in his chair. "Then I'm definitely not sitting there."

The flush on Ami's cheeks had gone to red. She clenched her fists, then hurled herself at me. "Why are we thrice-cursed fighting about every fucking thing every minute?" she shouted, pounding on my chest while I tried to hold her off my injured arm.

"Ami, stop," I said, keeping my tone gentle, trying to soothe her. She wasn't hitting me hard. In fact, she'd already sagged against me, fingers digging into my shirt as she held on, sobbing softly. I wrapped my good arm around her, ignoring the ache in the injured one in favor of the sweet delight of having her bosom crushed against it. "Ami, my Ami, my sun," I murmured, kissing her hair and holding her against me. I reveled in holding her, even as I kicked myself for having upset her yet again.

"I just wanted to have a nice dinner," she hiccupped. "I wanted things to be pretty."

"They are pretty. It's lovely. I'll sit wherever you want me to."

"No," she said miserably, face pressed into my chest. "You're right. It was thoughtless of me. I just..." She let out a long breath.

"What?" I urged. When she stubbornly shook her head, I levered the hand between us to lift her chin. Her eyes huge in her face, she looked fragile and vulnerable. Heartbreakingly beautiful. "Tell me, my sun."

"I just really miss you," she whispered. "I miss *us*, how we used to be."

I groaned, losing everything to her, as I'd done all along—even before I ever knew her. And I was kissing her, lush mouth soft and sweet under mine, then parting and taking me into her heat. I devoured her, frustrated that I could only hold her with one hand, but using that to cup her head and hold her still so I could drink her in. I'd been starved for the taste of her, for the silk of her hair between my fingers and the delicate curve of her skull in my palm.

She returned the kiss with increasing heat, whimpering my name, straining on tiptoes to reach me, so I let go of her long enough to pick her up. Even one-handed I could easily lift her, scooting her onto the table. She pushed aside the place settings and something crashed, shattering.

"Wait," I said.

"Fuck whatever it was," she panted. "Don't you dare stop."

~ 12 ~

SHE'D TUGGED MY shirt loose from the belt and had her hands on my chest, raking me with those deceptively rounded nails. I hissed, pushing between her legs and no more able to stop than if I were a wild and rutting beast. Every moan and whimper of hers fired my blood. She wrapped her legs around me, vising me in place, but the velvet mass of her skirts got in the way.

"Put your arms around my neck," I told her, and she complied, deliciously yielding. No longer needing to brace her, I yanked down the pretty neckline of her gown, freeing her naked breasts. A growl tore out of me, a sound of base need. Round and fair, pink nipples so tightly drawn up with her arousal that the areolae barely showed, the sight of her breasts shoved me over the edge of reason. Bracing a hand under the curve of her lower back, I feasted on those perfect breasts and fantastically hard nipples.

She arched back, offering herself to my mouth, her mewls firing me onward as I licked and bit at her. With her hands in my hair, she hung on, chanting my name and incoherent encouragement. At last she bent so far back her head touched the table, so I let her relax onto it, a feast for my lust. Her hair spilled like liquid fire over the dark wood, her skin impossibly fair against the deeper hues, her turgid nipples and swollen mouth beacons of flushed pink. Like her sweet cunt would be.

I had to see it, to expose her, taste her, have her. Pushing up her skirts, finding volumes of lace underskirts in different shades of violet, I parted her slim white thighs. Found her naked beneath. Rose-gold framing her pinkness. Hot. Slick.

Needing the taste of her with the desperation of a drowning man, I pushed her knees wide and fell on her, drinking in the sea salt sweetness of her body. The delicate folds of her sex slid under my tongue, her urgent cries driving me on. She climaxed, crying out my name in a hissed wail that sounded like anguish, her passage clamping on the finger I'd thrust inside her. She shuddered under my hands and I held her tight, loving the way she came apart for me, loving her cries of despairing pleasure as I drove her up again, not letting her down from the peak but pushing her further and harder.

When she was close, when she strained and struggled against me, panting as she begged, I freed my cock and drove it home. She climaxed around me, so primed that being filled undid her. Convulsing in the orgasm, she arched, arms thrown over her head in sensual abandon, eyes half-closed and mouth contorted as she cried out. I filled my hand with her breast, pinching the nipple hard so she writhed, calling for more. Her legs clamped so tightly around my hips there was no chance I could slip out, not to mention the way she milked my cock with her internal muscles.

My Ami might look angelic, but she possessed an uncanny mastery of the sensual skills. Another gift from the goddess of love. I slowed, stroking into her and savoring the way she enveloped me, so warm, an embrace like coming home. She watched me now through slitted lids, blue burning through the lace of fire, her moans like purrs. I bent over her, taking her nipple in my teeth and flicking my tongue that way that drove her crazy. She grabbed my head, bringing my mouth to hers, sucking my tongue in and biting hard enough to draw blood.

I snarled, losing what little gentleness I'd been able to muster. Holding her in place, pounding into her, my vision blurred into a red haze. A whirl of jeweled stars exploded in my brain, and with a shout of near agony, I wrenched my mouth from hers, sinking my teeth into the vulnerable curve of her neck. The climax vised through me, a rumbling thunder of need that rattled and rocked me.

Holding onto her like a drowning man, I dropped into oblivion.

THE PAIN IN my arm finally made me move. Trapped between us, the still-bruised flesh and knitting bones protested being pinned. Reality crashed back with it. I'd fucked the Queen of Avonlidgh on the grand table in the main hall of Windroven. An abysmally bad decision, even for me.

As if there'd been any thinking involved.

I groaned for my stupidity and started to lift myself, but Ami held on, imprisoning me in a web of white limbs and velvet like a midnight sky. "Not yet," she murmured and kissed my temple. "I'm not ready for this to end." She flexed her hips, inner muscles squeezing my sensitive post-come cock almost painfully.

A harsh laugh escaped me. "The servants might come in."

"They'd better not. I threatened to send them out into the blizzard if they so much as cracked the door."

I lifted my head, levering up enough to see her face, despite her grumbling protests. "You planned this."

She returned my accusing stare evenly. "I hoped."

I dropped my forehead against hers, then had to kiss her, with her enticing mouth right there. "We can't keep doing this," I scolded her, even as I fell again and again into kissing her. My arm throbbed and I didn't care. I never wanted to leave the sweet embrace of her body.

Which was a real problem, as I had to.

"Why not?" she was saying, holding on and finding my mouth when I tried to pull away. "This is good. This is everything. Why can't we have this?"

One of us had to put a stop to it. "Because my arm hurts like hell."

"Oh!" She immediately let me go. I slipped out of her, grabbing for a linen to catch our fluids. Once again I contemplated the horrific possibility that I might have planted my seed in her clearly fertile soil. She steadfastly refused to take precautions. Always I resolved not to fuck her again. Always I failed in that resolve with a pitiful lack of self-discipline. When we'd first become lovers, she'd been pregnant with the twins. She'd even used that to coax me, a low-life criminal, into taking her lovely body, saying I couldn't get her pregnant. Then she'd been healing from labor. Then, somewhere along the way, she seduced me into fucking her again, only laughing when I cautioned her that any child of ours would be a bastard.

Not what people would think, that the belle of Ordnung and darling of the Thirteen Kingdoms flaunted convention so carelessly. And yet also so very Ami.

"Are you all right?" she asked. "Ash?"

"I'm fine. Here." I gave her a clean cloth, a bad idea as I had to look in her direction. She sat on the edge of the table, dark skirts mounded around her, one knee drawn up so her pussy showed pink and open, beautifully framed. She hadn't fixed her dress either, so her breasts flowed generously over the dusky velvet, bite marks and scratches showing clearly on her fair flesh, particularly the purpling imprint of my teeth at the juncture of neck and shoulder. I rubbed a hand over my head. I'd totally lost control in my lust, yet again.

"I know that look," Ami said coolly, cleaning herself without any hint of shyness. "You better not be about to apologize."

"I hurt you."

"No more than usual," she replied crisply, then jumped off the table when I winced, pressing my hand over my eyes. "Ash." She wrapped her hands in my shirt, making me face her. "How many times do I have to tell you I like it?"

I touched the deep bite at her neck, summoning the healing energy, and she yanked away, dancing back. "No way. No healing the marks."

"Ami," I protested. "Don't be ridiculous, let me fix it. It'll show. People will see."

"Good." Her eyes flashed with satisfaction and she patted the mark, then lifted her breasts to survey the others. "I like having your marks on me. It's not something wrong that needs to be 'fixed.'" She began tucking her breasts back into their velvet nest, and I watched, helplessly rapt.

"I hope I didn't ruin your dress."

"Why do you always worry about my stupid dresses? They don't matter to me. You're always trying to fix the things that aren't important and ignoring what is."

"All right." I had no doubt she was correct. I'd always had a gift for making bad situations worse. "What is so important that I'm ignoring then?"

"Us!" She nearly shrieked it. "What we have together."

"We can't be together, Ami," I told her in a low voice. "We decided."

"Did we?"

"You know we did."

"I'm not so sure of that." Calming herself, she ran her fingers through her disheveled hair, plucking out the few remaining star pins. I picked up a couple scattered on the floor and handed them to her. "I'll just leave it down," she said, tossing them on the table. "My hair's at this weird in-between stage where it's so long that it gets in my way, but not quite long enough to braid or stay put up, even without you tearing at it, and—what?"

"What do you mean you're not so sure of that?" I said, sounding reasonably rational, which I wasn't. Since my throat was dry, I poured some wine into a crystal goblet. The other one had been what broke, so I gave the intact one to her and retrieved my mug from by the fire. "You sent me away."

"I let you go," she corrected. "Because you said you wanted to leave."

I took a deep breath. And, thrice curse it, refilled my already empty mug. Glorianna give me patience. "What I want doesn't matter. You and I know this has to end sometime."

"I don't know any such thing." She tossed her hair defiantly. "I hear you natter on about it, but you've never given me one good reason why."

I gritted my teeth. "I have so. You don't listen. To me or to anyone."

"Then tell me again. Right now. We love each other. Explain to me why that's not enough for you."

"It's not about me!" I gripped the mug so hard I thought the metal might give under my hand. "Love isn't some cure-all.

People can love each other and it still destroys them. Better we end this sooner, before we cause irreparable damage."

"Damage to who and what?" She demanded.

I shook my head, unable to explain the hugeness of it, growling at her, incoherent with all those things I could never explain.

"Won't you talk to me, Ash?" Ami asked, in a much softer tone. She eased closer, her hand out, like she might with a wild dog. She laid her fingers on me, gazing up with eyes full of compassion. "Trust me with this. What is this terrible thing that might happen? Is this about your parents?"

I put my hand over hers, pressing her hand to my heart, still unable to find the words. I couldn't escape that gaping sense of vulnerability, of never being able to explain to Ami how my father's love had killed my mother, how I'd been so bent on avenging him that I left my mother alone and unprotected. I'd loved her with all my being and I'd let her die, too.

I must have been disoriented, because it felt like the stones moved under my feet. Except that Ami flattened her mouth into an unhappy line, glancing at the ceiling. Something muttered in the background of my mind, a lonely howl beneath the roaring of the Mornai storm. The scent of scorch and decay wafted past—but in my mind, because the candle flames stayed straight and serene.

"Glorianna save us," I whispered, reflexively drawing Her circle in the air.

Ami inclined her head. "I've certainly been asking Her to. Though you might appeal to Moranu—I suspect awakening dragons falls to the goddess of magic and shapeshifting."

~ 13 ~

"WHY DIDN'T YOU tell me the dragon was awake enough to shake the castle?" I demanded for the third time, bolting the delicious, if lukewarm, meal as fast as possible. Ami had pleaded hunger and pointed out that I'd be more reasonable with a full belly. Since I knew I was feeling far from reasonable, and some time to cool my wildly stirred emotions couldn't hurt, I'd agreed. I had to admit, food helped a great deal to take that edge of desperation away.

"What could you have done about it, Ash?" Ami replied with some impatience. It took me a moment to realize she meant the dragon. "Up until last night, you were on the verge of dying."

"You should have told me the moment I was lucid." I should have figured out before now that the howling and muttering in my thoughts came from outside my nightmares. If I weren't so fucked in the head, I might have realized sooner. Some warrior I was, unable to discern the shrieking of his inner demons from the outer ones.

"Arguably I'm still waiting for that moment to come," she replied sweetly.

"Cute." I pushed back my chair and checked the draw of my short blade.

"What are you doing?" She frowned at me suspiciously.

"I've eaten, as directed, and now I'm going down to check out the tunnels."

"Oh no, you are not, mister. You're going back to bed."

I raised a brow at her. It would be better to have my sword, though I couldn't wield it well with that hand. Not as well as the short blade, but having the extra length might be worth the tradeoff in loss of dexterity. Dragons were big, so precision might not be as important as a bit more distance. I'd better get the sword.

Ami had stood, wrapping her hand in my belt and yanking me to her by the hips before I took a step. "Did you hear me?"

"I'm not Astar to be sent off to my room. Have Graves or any of the men gone to investigate?"

She looked aside and released me. Then followed when I kept walking. "No, I ordered them not to."

"Ami." I tried to keep my voice gentle, much as I wanted to shout at her for her foolishness. "Danger doesn't disappear just because you ignore it."

She snorted inelegantly. "This from the king of denial."

"What does that mean?"

"Give it a little thought." She leveled me with a fierce glare. "Come back when you want to have an actual conversation about your feelings."

I wasn't at all sure how we'd gone from discussing an awakening dragon making the stones of Windroven shake beneath our feet to something as irrelevant as my feelings. Having no reply, I said nothing.

"Well, I guess that non-response says everything," Ami commented. "At least take Graves with you. Maybe Skunk and some of the other men."

"I'll do better on my own. Faster." Plus I'd learned a few

mind-tricks in Annfwn about hiding my presence. The skilled practitioners could shield a whole group, but I was far from skilled. Ami followed me into her rooms. "Where did you put my sword?"

She pointed to one of the side chambers, where I found my leathers and other equipment, cleaned and neatly stacked. I eyed the leathers dubiously. Better to wear those, but I doubted I could get into them on my own. Glancing at Ami, I found she stood with arms folded, a stubborn tilt to her chin. "I'm not helping you with this fool's errand," she informed me.

"I understand. The leathers would protect me better, but I can do without."

She gave me the look of complete exasperation normally reserved for Willy and Nilly at their most impossible. Then threw up her hands and looked to the sky. "Why did you have to make me love *this* man?" It seemed Glorianna gave her no good answer because Ami leveled a defiant glare on me again. "Fine, I'll help you into your leathers, *after* I put on mine. I'm going with you."

"You absolutely are not."

"I'm not Stella, to be told what to do," she neatly threw my words back at me.

"Stella listens about as well as you do," I muttered.

Ami was already digging her leathers out of a cabinet in the next room. I'd never noticed there was a series of chambers, one leading into the next, with storage and another room with a bed in it. "Is this where you've been sleeping?"

"Mostly I've been sleeping in that chair next to the bed. But last night, once your fever broke, yes, I came in here, so I wouldn't disturb you."

"I'll sleep in here tonight. You should have your own bed

back."

She gave me an opaque look, but didn't reply directly. She simply turned around, lifted her hair and presented me with her back. "Laces, please."

It wasn't easy, one-handed, but she stood patiently as I plucked at them. Though I'd just had her, emptied myself in her in spectacular fashion, the familiar sight of her flawless skin through the parting velvet affected me as always. Perhaps because she'd torn down some of the walls between us, or because I'd lost some essential strength of will battling the nightmares and fever, this time I gave in to the crippling need to touch her.

I traced the line of her spine from the nape of her neck down between her winged shoulder blades, into the valley of the small of her back, and just to the top of her sweetly curved buttocks. Then yanked my hand away, lest I be tempted to do more. She looked over her shoulder at me, just as she had at Lianore. "I've missed you, Ash," she said, her voice throaty.

"I've been right here."

She shook her head. "No, you haven't. You were physically here, but *you* withdrew deep inside. You've been pulling further and further away from me since we left Annfwn. Do you miss it that much?"

"It's not that."

"Then what is it?"

I shook my head. "We've talked this to death already."

I expected a flare of anger, but she only studied me. "That's the thing. You think we have, but we've only talked around it."

"Well, we're not having some heart-to-heart conversation now. I'm going to assess the situation in the tunnels."

"Fine, fine." She dropped the gown, leaving it in a puddle on the floor, and stretched, gloriously naked. Then bent over to pull on the leather pants, knowing full well what the sight would do to me. Cursing her and Glorianna both, I turned away to at least get my own pants on without her help, lest she see the evidence of my helpless need for her, and use it to distract me again.

WE WENT THROUGH the silent kitchens, lit only by the fires under the baking ovens, the air warm and full of sugary spices. Cakes and other delights were arrayed on the counters, in various stages of assembly and decoration.

"Are you expecting an army for the Feast of Moranu?" I asked Ami.

She rolled her eyes at me. "When I say Windroven is virtually empty, that means only a hundred or so people are on the mountain. So, yes, we'll need a lot of cakes for the party tomorrow night. I invited everyone."

"Everyone?" I lifted a brow at her.

"Everyone," she repeated firmly. "The Three belong to us all equally, queen or milkmaid." She gave me an arch look. "Or Tala part-blood ex-convict."

I didn't rise to her bait, simply allowed her to lead the way through the cellar storerooms and into the labyrinth of tunnels beneath the castle. She hadn't worn her fighting leathers, acquired for our journey to rescue Stella from her abductors, since we'd left Annfwn. Besides the fact that they hugged her figure adorably, highlighting the sway of her hips and the play of muscle in her curving thighs and tight ass, they brought back a wealth of memories of those weeks together. Riding and camping. Me teaching her to use a knife. Ami in the firelight.

Fierce. Exhausted. Weeping over her injured sister but working to save her life with practiced determination.

A lot of that time we'd been alone but for Astar, and he'd been much younger, a sleeping infant. It seemed so long ago in a strange way. So much had happened since. But we'd been united in our mission, newly reunited and flush with the joy of it. With her dusty from riding, wearing her leathers with her knife on her hip, none of us bathing for days on end, she'd become only a woman to me. My woman.

For long stretches of time, I'd forgotten entirely that she was a princess, daughter of the High King and soon to be queen in her own right. Then we'd left Annfwn and returned to the world—her world of castles, elaborate gowns, and holding court—and it had all come crashing back.

She said I'd withdrawn, and perhaps I had. Some of it, yes, had been to prepare myself for when we'd part again. The rest—

Something howled in me, scraping over my nerves, hollowing my heart. Though it still sounded like my own pleas, begging for a mercy that never came—enough that I nearly staggered from the onslaught of memories—I could separate it this time. Not me. Not my thoughts and pained memories. The dragon.

~ 14 ~

"DO YOU HEAR that?" I asked Ami.

She cocked her head, listening intently. "I hear the surf beyond the walls, and the howl of the Mornai winds. But nothing from the volcano. Did you feel it move?"

"No. It's a sound on another level. I thought you might sense it, like you did the shadow guardians on the pass to Annfwn."

She shook her head, the tail she'd tied her hair into bouncing. "I lost pretty much all of that once Stella was born. The only pieces I have left seem to be tied to her. What does it sound like?"

"Like when I hear what the horses are feeling." I studied the branching tunnels. This far down they weren't as even, not neatly carved out for human use. These were made by the flows of lava and venting of steam. Sweat beaded at my temples and ran down my back. At the edges of my senses, the dragon roared, flaming through nightmares. "You go on back up," I told her.

"Sure!" she said brightly. "If you're coming, too."

I growled in frustration and she only beamed at me, all innocent amiability. "Fine, but pull your knife. Torch in the other hand. Stay behind me."

"Yes, sir." Snippy, but she complied.

I drew my sword, sorely wishing I could have a blade in each hand. Following the siren call of the dragon's pain, I led us through a series of tunnels, descending through air that grew more sere, stinking of gases from beneath the earth, and of decay on a psychic level. It stung my nostrils, burned in my brain, and heated my lungs, making me want to breathe out the fire again.

Or that was the dragon, muttering in my mind.

More than once I started to say we should turn back, if only for Ami's sake. Her face was flushed, sheened with sweat, but every time I looked back to check on her, she returned my gaze with fierce determination. She wouldn't go back without me. And I couldn't make myself stop.

The dragon drew me onwards, a compulsion below thought. I could no more resist than I could if this were one of the nightmares. I had no idea what I hoped to find, what I expected to do about the dragon, but I had to go on.

Something lunged at me out of the dark tunnel ahead, launching from some ledge above. My sword met it, spearing it through the chest with its own momentum. Though I'd cleaved it cleanly through the heart, it continued to flail, swiping and scrabbling with its claws, fangs snapping. I stomped a booted foot on its lower jaw, shoving its head back, then cleaved the head from the body in one clean stroke.

I took a moment to listen, to survey the shadows ahead for movement, then checked Ami. She'd crouched behind a rock outcropping, but straightened when I nodded all clear. Gripping her knife, she held out the torch, studying the creature which still scrabbled about aimlessly, teeth snapping at nothing.

"That's like those wolf things that attacked us," she said.

"I thought so, too. Not exactly a wolf. Some kind of cross with a reptile. The fur is nearly like the armor plating of scales."

"It's not alive, is it?" she whispered.

"No. No more than any of *Deyrr*'s creatures are." Its presence here explained some of the psychic stink.

"We have to burn it."

"Easily enough done, down here." I sheathed my sword and grabbed one of the flailing hind legs. "Watch my back, would you?"

"Always," she replied as if it were a vow, with a smile that warmed my heart.

Kicking the slavering head ahead of me, I dragged the carcass back to a rent in the tunnel that opened onto a pit with a radiant pool of lava below. I kicked the head into it, watching it sink with some satisfaction, then pushed the carcass after it. I'd have liked to hurl it in there, but a one-armed man had to take what he could. If only I could destroy the demons of my past as easily.

"Ash!"

I pulled my sword and put Ami behind me. Two more of the creatures charged us. One took a stroke to the throat but kept coming, latching onto my leg. I cleaved the head off the other, then did the same to the one biting me.

"Foul creatures," I swore. "Good thing they're slow."

"Slow? It bit you!"

"Not badly. Nothing like the one that got my arm. The leathers took most of the damage, so I'm glad you helped me get them on." Ami didn't smile back this time, looking furious and afraid.

"They're slow," I repeated, shoving the carcasses into the pit to follow their comrade. "That's what *Deyrr*'s magic does. It animates them, but nothing like a self-willed creature has. They don't have the intelligence to fight together. I noticed that when they attacked the sleighs."

"Oh, you noticed that, did you?" She sounded coolly incredulous. Better annoyed than afraid though.

I tossed her a grin, wiping my hands off on my thighs. The bite wound oozed a little blood, but was solidly in the meat of the muscle. It hadn't had time to chew down to the bone. "I don't know how or why these creatures are here. They stink of *Deyrr*, but don't have a clear mission."

She gazed down the tunnel. "Except maybe to keep us away from the dragon."

"Maybe that, yes."

"Then how are we going to let it out?"

The dragon wasn't much farther down, but I'd come close enough to learn all I needed to. It thrashed in nightmares, no closer to escaping them than I was to mine. Getting closer to it wouldn't do any good and would only put Ami at risk. "I don't think we can."

"What do you mean? Dafne let the one at Nahanau out."

"Yes—through the top of the volcano. Castle Windroven is in the way here. Like a cork in a bottle. I thought maybe if the dragon was awake enough, we could coax it out a side vent. But I can feel it in my head. It needs someone else to fully waken it, to show it the way."

"How awful." Ami's gaze searched the passage behind me, glimmering with her natural compassion. A sensitive and generous heart in my Ami.

"I've sent it some healing energy, to soothe it."

"I didn't know you could do that."

"Our secret." I smiled at her wearily. That effort had taken the last of my remaining energy. I might heal faster than non-Tala, but not that fast. Especially not with what I'd given the dragon. I had to admit that I couldn't fight off many more of the creatures.

"Then have you seen enough—can we go back?"

"Yes." Shadows smudged the hollows under her cheekbones and around her eyes.

Ami led the way and I followed, sword drawn and walking backwards to keep an eye on any attackers from behind. "I'll write to Andi and Ursula about it. Dafne, too," she said. "Maybe they can send someone to help the dragon."

"Good. In the meanwhile, I want to wake some of the men to close off access to these tunnels. We've been lucky so far, but I don't want to risk it."

"Agreed," Ami said with some fervency. "I don't want those creatures getting into the castle proper."

I grunted agreement. Slow as they were, they could do considerable damage, especially to the children.

"I still have the building schematics Dafne found in the library here," she said when we reached the kitchens. "We can use those to direct the men where to close everything off. I'll get those while you rouse the men."

"You should go to—"

"Not until you do," she cut me off crisply. "And I'm queen here. This is *my* castle. I'll oversee the work, see to your wounds, and then *we* will go to bed. If we're lucky, we'll sleep for an hour or two before Willy and Nilly start getting into trouble."

~ 15 ~

NEITHER OF US stayed to oversee the work. Graves persuaded us that he could follow the plans as well as anyone, and that it would be an insult to hover. He also really wanted his queen out of the lower tunnels as fast as he could move her along without giving offense. While I sympathized with the man's difficulties, I figured he could handle her himself.

I'd proven I had no ability to do so.

Just as well, as I passed out while Ami was still cleaning my leg wound. I hadn't lost that much blood, but—as she informed me—I'd lost plenty to begin with and hadn't had the opportunity to make more.

At least it saved the argument about sleeping arrangements. Or rather, my losing consciousness so precipitously had resolved the argument in Ami's favor. I awoke in her bed, feeling as if a sound had brought me alert. High above, a clear blue winter sky showed searingly bright through the clerestory windows. The storm had finally abated. No more howling wind. Even the sea had quieted to a muted, regular crashing of waves.

And somewhere beneath it all, the dragon slept.

So did Ami, curled up against my side, her back to me like a cat, only her bright hair showing on the pillow. I put a hand on her waist, finding her warm and naked. So was I, and my morning erection ached in a counterpoint with my healing arm and leg, all somehow equally painful. Along with my heart—or whatever facsimile remained of the shriveled, scarred thing.

Somehow revisiting those nightmares, making myself walk away from Ami over and over, all had conspired to rip the scar tissue off the oozing, pus-filled well of my psyche. I thought I'd healed. In those silent days of manual tasks and fervent prayer, I'd immersed myself in the routine of the White Monks. Glorianna's light and love had filled me, chasing away the shadows.

But that had been no more than a bandage. Underneath the white robes, I'd been a mess of broken bones too scattered to mend, the ichor of the prison left to fester and turn me into one of them. A monster.

I'd been a fool to love Ami, to let myself have her—not because she was so far above me, but because I wasn't whole enough to love anyone. Didn't trust myself, I supposed.

"Ash?" Ami whispered. I pulled my gaze from the intense blue of the sky out the windows to find the same clarity in her eyes, watching me with caution and concern.

"I didn't remember these windows, from before," I told her, in lieu of asking what she'd seen to make her worry. "Or this bed, for that matter."

"I had them put in. So you could see the sky even with the shutters closed. And I thought you'd like this bed better, because it kind of looks like the forest."

I studied her, impossibly moved. "You planned for me to come back here all along?"

"Of course," she said simply. "I always wanted you here with me, if I could be enough for you. I know you'd be giving up other things. Maybe more important things."

"Nothing is more important to me than you are. I'm sorry if I made it seem otherwise." I reached up and smoothed the hair out of her face. "My sun."

A line formed between her brows. "I wish you wouldn't call me that."

"My love," I amended, and pressed a kiss to that line, smoothing it away. "But you should know—it was never you. You never blinded or burned me. It was always me, too afraid of what I wanted. I wanted you more than anything, and that wanting terrified me."

She pulled back a little, laying a hand on my stubbled cheek. "Are you talking to me?"

"I'm trying. I'm not good at it. Silence is… easier." And it always had been, I realized. The White Monks, the vow of silence, that had been the tourniquet. It stopped the life-threatening loss of blood, but keeping it tight for too long had nearly made me lose what mattered most in my life.

"I think I understand that," she answered. "I try to, anyway. But sometimes… sometimes your silence hurts me. I feel like you don't trust me."

A sound came out of me, involuntary, pain to match hers. And maybe an acknowledgment of that truth. "I don't want you to think less of me," I admitted.

"Oh, Ash," she breathed. "You are the strongest, bravest, most amazing person I've ever met. You lived through horrible things that would break most people."

"I think they did break me." My voice, always hoarse, choked up, and wetness touched my lashes. I tried to turn my face away, so she wouldn't see, but Ami's hand tightened, holding me while she levered up to kiss my eyelids.

"You're not broken," she whispered against me. "You're

loving and kind. You embody patience, with me and the bratlings. You love me even when I'm being impossible and emotional."

"I like that you rage and weep. It's who you are—a vivid and passionate person who's fully alive. Your way is better. You so freely express what I can't. Sometimes…" I took a breath, focused on the sky. "Sometimes I think I'm like the volcano, with a cork in it. All this feeling inside me, it's the lava that will explode out and burn everything around me to ash."

"That's not you." Ami kissed me, heating it, stirring the passion between us until I groaned. "You do express it—during sex."

"I… what?"

"During sex. You show me everything then. It's the one time you're not all guarded. That's part of why I like everything you do to me, no matter what. Because it's really you, showing me what's really inside."

I didn't know what to think of that. Those seemed to be the times I lost control, when I lost sight of the man I'd tried so hard to craft from the shards left of that imprisoned boy. "I don't like that idea, that who I truly am is someone who hurts you."

"You never hurt me, not really. That's the thing. Not during sex, anyway. You only hurt me when you pull away."

"I pull away because I think I'm not good for you."

"Because you think loving someone means destroying them."

I nearly protested, but… "Maybe," I finally said.

"But we already love each other, and we're not destroyed. We're better. I love you. Astar and Stella love you. You'd only destroy us by taking that away. We'd be lost without you."

"You asked me to go."

"No. And you claim I don't listen." She shook her head and sat up a little, making me look at her. "I never wanted you to go. I was trying not to be selfish and keep you with me against *your* wanting to go."

I searched her face, bemused. "I never wanted to go. I thought you wanted me to."

She sighed, raking back her hair. "What a pair we are. Flinging words back and forth and never getting the right message across. Will you explain to me why you think I wanted you to leave me, when you are the one person who keeps me whole in my heart?"

"Do I do that?"

"Yes. You alone have never been dazzled by my face, my body. You tell me the truth—when you talk to me."

"Ami." Reverently, I reached up and touched her face, then slid my fingers through the enticing silk of her hair. "I'm eternally dazzled by you. I can't think straight when you smile at me. You know this."

"Maybe—but I don't agree on the thinking straight. You don't let me sway you, even when I try my best."

I laughed, a scrape of sound. "You sway me all the time."

"Do I? Then let me sway you now." She kissed me. "Stay with me. Don't ever leave me. Be with me always."

"Ami…" I tried, but she drank in the sound, making a hmm of pleasure. Reinforcing my grip on her shoulder, I set her away from me and sat up. "I can't do that."

"Aha." She sat up, too, folding her arms over her naked bosom. "So much for my power over you. Why not? You said you don't want to leave me."

"I don't want to." I scrubbed a hand over my face. "But we

can't be together forever. You know this."

"I don't know it. By Glorianna, you're going to explain this to me."

"You are the Queen of Avonlidgh."

"I'm well aware."

I shook my head in frustration. "You have obligations! To the throne of Avonlidgh, and to the High Throne, should it come to that. You have to marry a man of equal—or better— rank."

"I don't care about that."

"You have to care—you're a queen, not some dairy maid."

"Don't talk to me like I'm empty-headed." She said it quietly, warning in her tone.

"I know perfectly well you're not empty-headed," I snapped. "You're the smartest woman I've ever met, you're just foolish when it comes to me."

"You were doing well until that last bit. Ash—I am not a fool about you. I'm smart enough to know that I'm my best self with you. Glorianna laid Her hand on you and sent you to me. Now that I know you don't really want to leave me, I'm not letting you go. Ever. Chew on that."

Her decisive nod was mitigated somewhat by the luscious bounce of her breasts, but I managed not to smile. Or reach for her. No turning to sex to blunt the raw edges. Talk. Talk this out. "If you marry, your husband will not want me around."

"Easily solved: I won't marry anyone but you."

"You can't marry me!"

She shrugged a little. "Only because you haven't asked."

"What are you talking about?"

"At Ordnung, we discussed this. I said then I wouldn't marry anyone but you and you said that you hadn't asked me." Now she looked away, blinking rapidly.

I felt as if I'd been kicked by a horse: stunned, momentarily dizzy. We hadn't discussed it. She'd been in a strategy meeting with her sisters and I'd only attended because Ami insisted. At least that way I could keep an eye on her. "That wasn't about us." I felt my way through the words. "You were just saying that, to support Her Majesty, and I returned the joke in kind."

"No," she replied with exaggerated patience. "I said that because I want you to be my husband. Then I waited for you to ask me, like you seemed to want to. And then you never did. You wouldn't even dance with me—not at the coronation ball, not at Castle Avonlidgh."

"Ami…" I felt wrecked. So much I'd done wrong. "I wouldn't dance with you because I can't dance."

Her mouth fell open slightly. "Oh, Ash… *This* is your answer?"

"And I can't ask you to marry me," I continued doggedly. "You're a queen and I'm an ex-convict."

"Is that the only reason?"

"It's a pretty fucking big reason."

She glared, no longer so watery. "If I'm queen, I make the law. I can marry who I like."

"You're still subject to the High Queen's law."

"You think Essla wouldn't back me on this? Harlan is her consort and maybe there are good political reasons for him to stay that way, but she won't marry anyone else, either. I'll get her to make you into a duke or something, if that's what you need."

I shook my head, trying to clear it. "The Duchess of Lianore offered to dub me Lord Sousbois."

Ami smiled. "It's a pretty place. You'd like it."

"It's not so easy as that."

"It is that easy, Ash." She framed my face with her hands. "Just let me love you. Let yourself love me and everything else will fall into place."

"Love doesn't solve everything."

"No." She kissed me. "But it makes everything worthwhile."

I sank into her, into the kiss and into the silken sweetness of her embrace. In the soft light of morning, I let myself love her as she'd asked, showing her with caresses and all the rawness in me, how very worthwhile that could be.

~ 16 ~

WE GATHERED, THE four of us, to exchange gifts in the last of the light of that day. Astar and Stella, of course, had been going mad with anticipation for theirs. And they wouldn't last through the vigil until midnight. Ami declared that tradition could wait on them growing up more, and for now we'd share opening presents as a family, in the late hours of afternoon of the shortest day of the year.

That worked fine for me, though it shortened my preparation time. Next year, I'd be ready. Next year at Windroven. Since I knew where I'd be, for the first time since I escaped that prison.

And for the first time, I realized that maybe part of me had never escaped, and it was past time to let him out. I'd found continuity, my own home, in Ami and at Windroven. I could be safe here. And it was time to embrace the new, letting the past fall away.

Astar loved the sword I'd carved for him. It would do until I could get him a better one. Because my parents had always given me intangible gifts instead of material things they couldn't afford, I also gave Astar a scroll, explaining that it was the gift of sword lessons.

Ami gave both Astar and Stella pretty toys, and—to my

surprise—she also gave promises—scrolls tied with ribbons. This one her love. This one hugs for the asking. More to call in favors of games to play or a willing ear to listen to their troubles.

I'd cut up my White Monk's robes, to make a cape for Stella. A cloak of invisibility, I told her, so she could wrap up in it, be quiet, and not have to feel what everyone else felt. With it I gave her a scroll promising lessons in that too, and in healing. She accepted it gravely, stretching up to kiss my cheek, while Astar whooped around the room, swinging the wooden sword in wild circles.

Making those had left me little time, so I gave Ami the scroll I'd made for her with an apology.

"Why apologize?" she asked. "The kids like toys to play with, but Moranu is the goddess of the intangible. It's traditional to give the gift of a promise, or something else that isn't a material item."

I gazed back at her, bemused. "I thought my parents only did that because they were poor."

She leaned in and kissed me. "Maybe sometime you can tell me stories about them. Anything you feel you can, I want to hear."

"About that—this is one of those stories," I told her, handing over the scroll. It had been terrible to write out, leaving a pall of illness behind. Just the pus, oozing out. Curiously, after I finished, I felt lighter, as if the act of telling the story had cleansed that infection. I'd made two copies: one for her, and one to burn at midnight.

Ami clutched it so tightly she dented the scroll, her eyes full of emotion. "Thank you," she whispered.

"There's more. It might take time to tell you all of it, but I want you to know. So here is this gift." I unrolled it and showed her. I written one word on it. *Trust.* And she smiled to see it.

"One more." I glanced wryly at the kids, Stella now the lion cub batting at the thrusts of Astar's practice sword. "Not exactly a romantic setting, but…" I went down on one knee.

"Oh, Ash."

I had to calm the frantic battering of my heart, speaking slowly to get the words past the scarring. "Amelia, my love, my sun in the best of all possible ways. Will you be my wife?"

"Yes." She caught her breath on a sob. "Yes. We'll have a big wedding."

"I don't care about the formalities. I'm already yours, if you'll have me."

I stood to kiss her, but she reached for the remaining scroll she'd brought, holding it against her breasts with a sly smile.

"Oh, I'll have you, all right, but we're going to do it right, for all the world to see. And this is a start." She handed it to me and rang a bell.

I laughed as I read it—then resigned myself as the quartet of musicians came in and set up. Ami held out her hands and I took them.

"Put one hand here, and the other here," she instructed. "Listen for the music. One, two, three. One, two, three."

Just before the clock struck midnight, Ami and I threw our dark secrets into the fire. She'd never done that part of the tradition, but enthusiastically embraced it. She and I spent the last dark hours of that year writing down all the things we wanted to leave behind. Holding hands, we burned them, consigning them to ash.

Then we collected the sleepy twins and took our votives to the big landing, where everyone had assembled. Graves and Skunk were there, and many other people I'd never seen before. All in their best finery. Even the lowest servants joined us, dousing the last of the castle lights as they did, standing on the ascending stairways if they couldn't crowd onto the landing. At the chime, we blew out the last of our candles, standing together in the dark. Beyond the great glass windows, the sparkling dark night resolved.

The second chime rang, and people began to relight their candles. I lit Stella's, her luminous eyes catlike and solemn, while Ami lit Astar's. Outside the windows, torches lit at the castle walls, then ran in a rapidly expanding circuit around all the turrets, then pouring down the winding road down the peak. Ami laughed with pure joy and the kids squealed, nearly forgetting their own candles.

"I so hoped the wind would stop long enough for this," Ami told me. "I really wanted to see it. For all of us."

"I understand why," I told her, cupping her cheek. In the brilliance of the moment, I didn't care who watched us. I kissed her, something rekindling inside me also, the light spreading throughout.

WITH WILLY AND Nilly safely back abed, we joined the party already well underway in the great hall. But they cleared the space for us, and so I led my love onto the dance floor, setting the pace and the tone for the coming year. I wore the clothes Ami had made for me herself, the deep greens of my calling as a healer, embroidered with leaves in ivory, pink, purple and bloodred. All of my allegiances in one.

Though the dance was far from perfect, I did my best. Looking down into Ami's radiant face, I realized that sometimes that's all right.

And that love, like fire, might burn and rage, but it also lit the dark night with hope. Which made it all worthwhile.

TITLES BY JEFFE KENNEDY

OTHER FANTASY ROMANCES

A COVENANT OF THORNS

Rogue's Pawn
Rogue's Possession
Rogue's Paradise

THE TWELVE KINGDOMS

Negotiation
The Mark of the Tala
The Tears of the Rose
The Talon of the Hawk
Heart's Blood
The Crown of the Queen

THE UNCHARTED REALMS

The Pages of the Mind
The Edge of the Blade
The Snows of Windroven
The Shift of the Tide
The Arrows of the Heart
The Dragons of Summer
The Fate of the Tala

THE CHRONICLES OF DASNARIA

Prisoner of the Crown
Exile of the Seas
Warrior of the World

SORCEROUS MOONS

Lonen's War
Oria's Gambit
The Tides of Bára
The Forests of Dru
Oria's Enchantment
Lonen's Reign

THE FORGOTTEN EMPIRES

The Orchid Throne
The Fiery Crown

CONTEMPORARY ROMANCES

Shooting Star

MISSED CONNECTIONS

Last Dance
With a Prince
Since Last Christmas

CONTEMPORARY EROTIC ROMANCES

Exact Warm Unholy
The Devil's Doorbell

FACETS OF PASSION

Sapphire
Platinum
Ruby
Five Golden Rings

FALLING UNDER

Going Under
Under His Touch
Under Contract

EROTIC PARANORMAL

MASTER OF THE OPERA E-SERIAL

Master of the Opera, Act 1: Passionate Overture
Master of the Opera, Act 2: Ghost Aria
Master of the Opera, Act 3: Phantom Serenade
Master of the Opera, Act 4: Dark Interlude
Master of the Opera, Act 5: A Haunting Duet
Master of the Opera, Act 6: Crescendo
Master of the Opera

BLOOD CURRENCY

Blood Currency

BDSM FAIRYTALE ROMANCE

Petals and Thorns

OTHER WORKS

Birdwoman
Hopeful Monsters
Teeth, Long and Sharp

Thank you for reading!

About Jeffe Kennedy

Jeffe Kennedy is an award-winning author whose works include novels, non-fiction, poetry, and short fiction. She has won the prestigious RITA® Award from Romance Writers of America (RWA), has been a finalist twice, been a Ucross Foundation Fellow, received the Wyoming Arts Council Fellowship for Poetry, and was awarded a Frank Nelson Doubleday Memorial Award. She serves on the Board of Directors for the Science Fiction and Fantasy Writers of America (SFWA) as a Director at Large.

Her award-winning fantasy romance trilogy *The Twelve Kingdoms* hit the shelves starting in May 2014. Book 1, *The Mark of the Tala*, received a starred Library Journal review and was nominated for the RT Book of the Year while the sequel, *The Tears of the Rose* received a Top Pick Gold and was nominated for the RT Reviewers' Choice Best Fantasy Romance of 2014. The third book, *The Talon of the Hawk*, won the RT Reviewers' Choice Best Fantasy Romance of 2015. Two more books followed in this world, beginning the spin-off series *The Uncharted Realms*. Book one in that series, *The Pages of the Mind*, was nominated for the RT Reviewer's Choice Best Fantasy Romance of 2016 and won RWA's 2017 RITA Award. The second book, *The Edge of the Blade*, released December 27, 2016, and was a PRISM finalist, along with *The Pages of the Mind*. The next in the series, *The Shift of the Tide* and *The Arrows of the Heart* came out in August, 2017, and October, 2018. A high fantasy trilogy, The Chronicles of Dasnaria, taking place in *The Twelve Kingdoms* world began releasing from Rebel Base books in 2018. The novella, *The*

Dragons of Summer, first appearing in the *Seasons of Sorcery* anthology, finaled for the 2019 RITA Award.

She also introduced a new fantasy romance series, *Sorcerous Moons*, which includes *Lonen's War, Oria's Gambit, The Tides of Bàra, The Forests of Dru, Oria's* Enchantment, *and Lonen's Reign.* She's begun releasing a new contemporary erotic romance series, *Missed Connections*, which started with *Last Dance* and continues in *With a Prince* and *Since Last Christmas.*

In September 2019, St. Martins Press released *The Orchid Throne*, the first book in a new romantic fantasy series, *The Forgotten Empires.* The sequel, *The Fiery Crown*, will follow in May 2021.

Her other works include a number of fiction series: the fantasy romance novels of *A Covenant of Thorns*; the contemporary BDSM novellas of the *Facets of Passion*; an erotic contemporary serial novel, *Master of the Opera*; and the erotic romance trilogy, *Falling Under*, which includes *Going Under, Under His Touch* and *Under Contract.*

She lives in Santa Fe, New Mexico, with two Maine coon cats, plentiful free-range lizards and a very handsome Doctor of Oriental Medicine.

Jeffe can be found online at her website: JeffeKennedy.com, every Sunday at the popular SFF Seven blog, on Facebook, on Goodreads and pretty much constantly on Twitter @jeffekennedy. She is represented by Sarah Younger of Nancy Yost Literary Agency.

jeffekennedy.com

facebook.com/Author.Jeffe.Kennedy

twitter.com/jeffekennedy

goodreads.com/author/show/1014374.Jeffe_Kennedy

Sign up for her newsletter here.

jeffekennedy.com/sign-up-for-my-newsletter